You Don't Know Me Like That

RUMOR CENTRAL

Also by ReShonda Tate Billingsley

Rumor Central

Published by Kensington Publishing Corporation

You Don't Know Me Like That
RUMOR CENTRAL

RESHONDA TATE BILLINGSLEY

Dafina KTeen Books
KENSINGTON PUBLISHING CORP.
http://www.kensingtonbooks.com

DAFINA KTEEN BOOKS are published by

Kensington Publishing Corp.
119 West 40th Street
New York, NY 10018

ISBN-13: 978-0-7582-8953-7
ISBN-10: 0-7582-8953-7
First Printing: October 2013

eISBN-13: 978-0-7582-8954-4
eISBN-10. 0-7582-8954 5
First Electronic Edition: October 2013

10 9 8 7 6 5 4 3 2 1

Printed in the United States of America

To my Divas,

Mya and Morgan

A Note from the Author . . .

When I started working for the *National Enquirer* tabloid magazine, I had no idea that it would send my imagination into overdrive and help me to one day create a young diva who blows up by dishing celebrity dirt. But I'm glad for that experience, because it helped shape the stories for the *Rumor Central* series.

I am loving the love you guys have shown for the series so far, and I hope that this second book delivers as well. Please tell a friend about the *Rumor Central* series (and tell your teachers, librarians, and everyone else to get it as well!).

In the meantime, let me say a gigantic thanks to my daughters, Mya and Morgan, especially Morgan, who constantly gave me feedback and input! Thanks to the rest of my family, my friends, my agent, Sara Camilli, my awesome editor, Selena James, and all the fab folks at Kensington.

Thanks to the terrific readers who pick up my books, tell others, and show me so much love. Big shout-out to all the teen book clubs that choose my books to discuss.

Thank you to the parents, teachers, librarians, and concerned adults who turn teens on to my books. I am so grateful to you.

I can't wrap without sending a huge shout-out to my social media followers. You guys keep me motivated, inspired, encouraged, and show me so much love! A thousand thanks.

Well, that's it for now. Make sure you hit me up and let me know what you think about the second book. Now, get to reading. The third book in the *Rumor Central* series is coming soon!

Much love,
ReShonda

You Don't Know Me Like That

RUMOR CENTRAL

Chapter 1

Divalicious!

I read the headline for what had to be the twentieth time. My fabulous photo covered the whole front page. I needed to call Alicia Keys and thank her for writing a song about me because This Girl Was On Fire!

Don't get it twisted. I already knew I was fabulous—shoot, I came out of my mama's womb fabulous—but this just proved it beyond any doubt. The fact that I was on the cover of the Entertainment section of *USA Today*—with a full spread—proved I was the hottest teen star in the country. And I hadn't had to act in one movie to get that title. In just three short months, I had become the go-to chick for all the latest celebrity gossip, dirt, and entertainment news. My show, *Rumor Central,* had exceeded everyone's expectations and had been picked up by several other cities. So, I was no longer just known all over Miami; I was now known all over the country. Next stop, the world!

"Really, Maya? How many times are you gonna read that article?"

"Don't hate," I said, taping the newspaper to the front of my locker despite school rules. My locker was in a prime spot right by the cafeteria, so all my classmates would see it as they made their way in for lunch. I turned to my best friend, Sheridan. "Can I help it that I'm divalicious?"

"Ugggh," Sheridan said, playfully rolling her eyes as she tapped away on her Samsung Galaxy III phone.

A few months ago, I would've had a problem with Sheridan's eye rolling. But that was then. This was now. We had settled our little beef. I'd gotten over the fact that Sheridan had pushed up on my boyfriend. And Sheridan had gotten over the fact that I had basically left her and the other members of the *Miami Divas* reality show high and dry when it came time to get my own show. Sheridan was able to forgive me because she knew if the shoe were on the other foot, she would've done the exact same thing. But the others—Shay, Bali, and Evian—they weren't so forgiving. Bali had gone back to Cuba. (His father sent him back after finding out he was involved in a vandalizing and theft ring.) But he made sure that he sent me a text every now and then reminding me how foul I was.

Evian and Shay were still walking around with attitudes. But screw them. Maya Morgan didn't need to beg anybody to be her friend.

"Hey, did you know you're trending on Twitter?" Sheridan said, tapping the screen on her phone.

"What?" I said.

"Yeah." Sheridan turned her phone around and pointed it at me so I could see. "See, *Rumor Central* is in the top ten trends."

"Wow," I replied. Sometimes we got a lot of people talking after a show aired, but I had never been a top trender before. "That's crazy. We usually don't get hype like that except when the show is airing live."

"Guess that newspaper spread is working," Sheridan said.

"I guess." I closed my locker, then thought I probably should get some type of book or tablet since I was heading to class. I opened the locker back up and pulled out my textbook.

Sheridan shrugged. "Well, you're doing something. Listen to what some of these tweets say: **'If you're not watching Maya, you're missing out,' 'Maya's got the dirt,'** and **'Can't wait to see what Maya's talking about tomorrow.'** "

One of my classmates walking by must have overheard us, because she stopped and said, "Oh, yeah, congrats on that." She pointed to Sheridan's phone. "You've been trending all week."

"How do I not know this?" I said, pulling out my own phone and going to Twitter. I clicked on and read some more of the tweets.

If you're not watching Rumor Central, u r missing out!

Rumor Central is the biz

Watch out, Wendy Williams; there's a new gossip girl in town.

All of them had the hashtag #RumorCentral and came from someone using the Twitter handle Rumor Central.

"Wow," I mumbled.

"Yeah, looks like your social media department is on top of things," Sheridan said.

"I know. And to think, I thought they were kinda whack. But as soon as I get into work this afternoon, I'm going to go give them major props."

"And a raise," she joked as we made our way to class.

As soon as I hit WSVV, the TV station where they filmed *Rumor Central,* I headed to Tamara Collins's office. She was the executive producer on my show and the one who called all the shots.

It was after five, so Tamara's secretary wasn't at her desk, so I just knocked on her office door.

"Hey, Tamara," I said, once she called for me to come in. I was always in awe whenever I went into her office. Talk about top of the line. Everything in here was first class—from the marble desk to the plush leather chairs. Her walls were covered with awards that I guess she'd won for her television shows, and pictures of everyone from Jay-Z to Justin Bieber. The only thing out of order was her cluttered desk.

"Hello, Maya. How was school today?"

"School was school." I shrugged as I walked in. I wasn't into my senior year like the rest of my classmates. Even though we were a private school, we still did the typical senior week, parties and events during homecoming—none of which interested me. I was on a whole different level than those busters at Miami High.

I plopped down in front of Tamara's oversized desk. She was sifting through a pile of papers on it. I smiled as I took in her BCBG suit. It was a new design that had just come out last week.

"I just wanted to swing by and give props to the social media department. They are on it."

She didn't look up from her desk. Obviously, she was searching for something. "Maya, what are you talking about?"

"I'm talking about Twitter."

"What about it?"

I guess she didn't know either. "*Rumor Central* is trending on Twitter. I didn't do it, so I just assumed the social media department did it."

She finally stopped and stared at me. "I don't see how that's possible. We just got rid of the old girl because she was so behind, she didn't even know what Instagram was."

I smiled. "Well, whoever took her place is definitely on his or her job."

She looked at me. "Yeah, that's just it. We don't have anyone working social media right now." She picked up the phone. "Let me call marketing. They usually don't leave until late." She punched in a number. "Hey, Sara, it's Tamara. Do you have anyone working on the publicity for *Rumor Central*?" She paused. "So, they're just doing PR and not social media?" She paused again, then shook her head. "Okay, thanks. Let me know when you get someone. I'd like to meet with him or her."

"So, what's up?" I asked when she put the phone back on the hook.

"Well, what's up is someone else is behind that Twitter trending. It's not us. Publicity was aware of it, and they were actually trying to find out who was behind it. Sara said they'd called you earlier to see if it was you."

I shook my head. "I didn't get a message, but no, it's not me."

Tamara smiled. "Guess it looks like you officially have a serious fan. He or she is going all-out."

"Wow, I guess I do," I said, a bright smile spreading across my face. "Wish we had someone like whoever is behind this on staff," I said. "Because if I'm trending above Kim Kardashian, I'm obviously doing something right."

"You know," Tamara said, cocking her head like she was thinking, "you may be on to something." She pressed the intercom. "Kelly, are you still here?"

"I'm here," her secretary said. "I just stepped away for a minute. But I am about to go. Do you need anything?"

"Yes, just for a minute. Can you come in here? I have someone I need you to find. Maya's superfan." She smiled my way. I grinned back at her. I had fans, I knew that, but this was taking things to a whole different level. But I guess that's what happens when you're divalicious like me!

Chapter 2

". . . And that's right, if you want the scoop, you know we're doing the digging. Until next time, holla at your girl."

The music came up in our spacious, trendy studio as Manny, our director, gave me the all clear. "Good job as always," he said.

I removed my earpiece and smiled. I wanted to say, "Tell me something I don't know," but I was going to play it cool, and so I just said, "Thanks."

I knew that show was going to be the bomb. I'd just broken the story about Chris Brown and Rihanna getting back together for the umpteenth time. In the beginning, people used to doubt if the gossip I delivered was legit, but in the three months I'd been on the air, they'd quickly learned that I wasn't in Miami's "it" clique for nothing.

I had just made it back to my office when Carl, the mail-room clerk, walked in.

"Girl, I think we need a separate office just to store all your gifts and fan mail. I mean, who even sends snail mail anymore? You'd think with social media, some of this stuff would fall off," he said, setting down a big basket of letters.

Since my show had been on the air, I'd been getting cards,

gifts. One of the football players from the University of Miami had even tried to date me. I talked to him on the phone a couple of times, but when he started trying to get me to go away for the weekend, I knew I needed to back off. Besides, I didn't want to do my baby Bryce like that. But I'd seen some of everything. That's because they were definitely feeling me.

"You ready to go?" My friend, Kennedi, had been sitting in my office waiting for me to finish taping. I really wish that I could've invited both her and Sheridan to this party tonight, but the two of them didn't get along—at all. They were my two best friends in the whole world and couldn't stand each other. So I was forced to do stuff with them one at a time. Tonight was Kennedi's night.

"I said, are you ready to go?" I dropped my scripts on my desk.

"Oh, sorry. Didn't hear you," she replied.

"What are you looking at anyway?"

"Well, I was just scrolling through Twitter, but then you started trending, and I got caught up reading it."

"I'm trending again?" I asked. "I was just trending yesterday."

"Yeah, well, you're trending today, also," she said.

"Dang, we really need to find the person who's behind that." Just then, my assistant, Ariel, walked in.

"Good show, Maya," she said.

"Thanks," I said. I don't know why these people expected anything less from me. Every show I did was going to be a good show.

"Hi," Ariel said to Kennedi.

"Hey," Kennedi said, not really looking up from her phone.

"So, do you need anything else from me?" Ariel asked.

Just then, it dawned on me; the more people we had trying to track down this person on Twitter, the better.

"Yeah, matter of fact, I need you to see if can you find out who set up the *Rumor Central* Twitter account," I said.

"The station didn't do it?" she asked.

Duh. "If they had, then I wouldn't be asking you to find out who did it, now would I?" I swear, sometimes I couldn't believe this chick was about to graduate from college.

Ariel had only been with me for a few weeks, but there was something about her that I just wasn't feeling. She was a senior at the University of Miami and working here as my assistant as part of some college work-study program. It's not that she didn't do her job. But you know how some people just give the vibe that they can't be trusted? That's how I felt with Ariel. She was a pretty girl—nothing to get excited about—but she always seemed to be lurking around, and it got on my nerves.

"The marketing department is working on it, but I thought you could try to track her down as well. If you find anything out, let Tamara know."

She nodded. "I'll get right on it."

"Thanks." She didn't move, so I said, "Anything else?"

She shifted nervously. "Well, I know I've only been here a month," she began stammering. "I was just wondering. . . . Everyone didn't get a big break like you. . . ."

I narrowed my eyes at her.

She quickly tried to clean that up. "Oh, I'm not saying that's a bad thing. I think it's great that you've had the opportunities that you have. I mean, you're good, so you deserve all the success you have. But well, I was kinda hoping you could take a look at my demo tape. And if you like it, maybe you could, ah, you know, put a word in for Tamara to let me fill in or do some fieldwork on your show."

It took everything in my power not to look at her crazy. I should've known. She wanted to be on air and probably had some resentment that here I was, at seventeen, with my own show, and she was, well, she was my assistant.

"I'm not sure what you'd like me to do, Ariel," I said.

"Just look at my tape. That's all. And let me know what you think."

"Okay," I lied. I didn't like horror movies, and just the thought of Ariel trying to be a reporter was enough to scare me.

She handed me the tape, which I just noticed was clutched in her hand. "I know you're busy, but if you'd look at it as soon as you can and let me know, I'd appreciate it."

I gave her a tight smile as I patted the tape. "As soon as I can."

"Okay, I'll let you go. Have a good day."

I just nodded. As soon as she was gone, Kennedi looked up from her phone. "That chick wants your job." She laughed.

"Who doesn't?" I said, gathering up my things.

"Are you gonna watch her tape?" Kennedi asked.

I turned up my lips, grabbed the tape, and dropped it in the trash.

Kennedi chuckled. "I didn't think so." She finally dropped her phone in her purse and stood.

I grabbed my jacket. "I'm not thinking about that for now. I'm off the clock. Let's roll."

Kennedi followed me to the door. "Girl, you are never off the clock. Just once, I'd like for us to go somewhere and chill and not get bombarded with folks asking for your autograph."

"Don't hate," I said, wiggling my petite hips. "That's now the story of my life!"

Chapter 3

I loved my life! A slammin' party last night. Red carpet tonight. It didn't get any better than this.

The flashing lights of the paparazzi lit up the night. I was in the front of the Olympia Theater, and there were people lined up along both sides of the velvet rope. I turned from camera to camera, flashing my fabulous smile.

"Maya, over here!" someone shouted.

I turned in his direction just as another photographer shouted, "Maya, this way." I struck yet another pose.

Normally, I would be the one waiting to interview celebrities, but since I was being honored tonight with a Young Achiever's Award, I was actually walking the red carpet. Yes, Maya Morgan was getting honored tonight with One Direction, Kanye West, and Taylor Swift. It didn't get any more fab than this.

"Well, if it isn't the gorgeous Maya Morgan."

"Hey, Terrance," I said, turning to greet the *Entertainment Tonight* reporter. It had been prearranged that I would stop and talk to Terrance, with his little cute self.

"Usually, you're over here with us," he said as his photographer zoomed in on me.

"Not tonight, babe," I said, tossing my perfectly styled Brazilian Blowout curls over my shoulders.

"You rockin' that dress," he said.

"Oh my God, is that a Valentino original?" his cohost, Giuliana, said.

"It is." She knew her stuff. My mom had shelled out a pretty penny for this dress. She loved my red carpet events and made it her mission to find the perfect dress for each event. And this royal blue Valentino original was no exception.

"You know you make me feel like such a slacker," Giuliana said. "When I was your age, I wasn't thinking about anything but boys and clothes."

"Oh, I still think about that." I laughed. "I just have to also include work."

They asked me a few more questions, then I wrapped things up and made my way over to Sasha, the girl my station had sent over to interview me.

Of course, I nailed that and was making my way inside when I ran into rapper and resident hood chick, Paula Olympia. I groaned because I knew this was not going to be pretty. I'd done a story last week about her little affair with a costar on the set of her new music video. It was news her new boyfriend didn't take too kindly, and he'd dumped her like he'd caught her twerking naked on Twitter.

Paula stepped closer to me and immediately side-eyed my security. I only had one guy, but he was pretty big. Mann made his way toward me.

"You don't have to send your whack bodyguard over here." She stepped closer. Her mini sequined dress was so tight, I was surprised she could move. One wrong move and her goodies would be all out in the open. "I'm not going to touch you. Yet," she threatened.

I held up a hand to let Mann know everything was fine. For now.

"Let me tell you something," Paula continued. "If you ever utter my name again, you will live to regret it."

"Well, sweetie," I said, pushing the train of my dress to the side just in case something did jump off, "you and your threats don't scare me. I don't make the news; I just report it."

She took a step closer and whispered in my ear. "That's not a threat, sweetie. It's a promise. This game you're playing is real."

I was happy to see Mann move in closer. "I'm just doing my job."

"Your job sucks."

"I'm sure you think that," I said. I wanted to tell her if she were faithful to her man, she wouldn't have to worry about any rumors getting out. But since I didn't need any drama jumping off on the red carpet, I just smiled.

"Excuse me," I said, pointing toward the door. "I need to get inside."

She didn't move. "Little girl, you're in the big leagues now. I'm not going to do anything to you; you're not worth it to me. But one of these days, you're going to cross the wrong person. You can't just play with people's lives and then expect to walk around like nothing is wrong."

I didn't understand why everyone was always mad at me because of this show. They were the ones that did the dirt. All I did was report it.

"You need to stick to football games and whatever else you little high school kids are into and stay out of grown folk's business," she spat.

"Are you finished?" I smirked. "Because I need to get inside and accept my award."

I saw a camera pointing our way, so I refused to get angry. Instead, I smiled wider and said, "By the way, I love that dress, Paula. It's so . . . festive." Then I stepped around her and her green Christmas tree–looking dress and headed inside.

"You okay?" Mann asked.

"I'm cool," I said. "Just another hater." I had known going in that this job wasn't going to be easy. But I'd made a name for myself digging up dirt, and I wasn't about to turn back now.

Chapter 4

I love me some him. That's all I could think as I stared across the small intimate table at Perry's Steakhouse. My boo had done it up good. He was taking me out to celebrate my award from last night since it was so late by the time I wrapped up. And to think he had almost let me get away.

That's right. Bryce and I broke up a few weeks ago because he let Sheridan fill his ear with a bunch of gossip. Yes, *that* Sheridan, my BFF. She was mad at the way the whole *Rumor Central* thing went down and tried to pay me back by kicking it with him.

Kennedi and a few of my other friends thought what she did was super foul and that I shouldn't forgive her, but Sheridan and I go way back, and I'm not going to let some boy come between us. Even a boy as fine as my boo. So I'd forgiven her, but I still kept one eye open. I'm no fool.

Bryce is the total package. His dad plays for the Miami Dolphins. He's going to go to the pros himself, but he's determined that he's going to college to get an education first. He's one of the only jocks in all honors courses and doesn't care about his friends giving him a hard time about it. He's fine, smart, independent, and rich. Just like I like them.

"What are you thinking about?" he asked me.

"Oh, nothing." I smiled. Bryce had the swag of Chris Brown, the looks of Drake, and the fun-loving personality of Nick Cannon. Oh, and did I mention he was rich? That meant he was everything I ever wanted in a boyfriend. So, he definitely deserved a second chance.

"Did you like your filet mignon?" he asked.

"I did," I said.

"But you barely ate it."

I frowned and pointed to the huge steak on my plate. "Look how big that meat is."

"It was the smallest one on the menu."

"It was delicious, but I don't keep this gorgeous figure by eating gigantic steaks." I laughed.

"And your figure is gorgeous," he said, running his eyes up and down my peach jumpsuit.

"What do you have for me?" I finally asked.

"What are you talking about?" he replied, looking all serious. "This dinner was your gift."

I stuck my bottom lip out in a playful pout. "You said you had something special for me to celebrate my award."

"You are so spoiled," he said, reaching into his pocket and pulling out a small blue box. That light blue was my favorite color.

"Tiffany's," I squealed, snatching the box. I opened it up. It was the necklace to match the bracelet he'd given me for my birthday. "You are the best," I said, jumping up and going over to his side of the table to hug him.

We sat back and laughed and talked some more, then he said, "You know, I really am proud of you."

I was just about to reply when two guys approached our table. They both wore baggy jeans and Southpole T-shirts. Talk about whack! One of them had long cornrows and the other had a red do-rag on his head. How did they even get in? They looked like they'd just stepped out of a bootleg rap video.

"Oh, wow! It is Maya Morgan," the one with the braids exclaimed.

I flashed a thin smile their way while Bryce just looked at them.

"I told you it was her," the other one said.

The braided dude stepped closer. That's when I noticed his apron in his hand. They must work in the back in the kitchen or something. "I'm Slim," he said. "This is my boy Heavy." That was the craziest thing I'd ever heard, because Slim was about three hundred pounds and Heavy looked like he couldn't weigh more than one hundred and twenty pounds.

"Dang, you're even finer in person," Slim said.

"Thank you," I said, keeping my thin smile.

Bryce wasn't smiling, though. I could tell he was getting really agitated.

"Wow, you are beautiful. You got a man?" Slim asked.

Bryce's fist balled up as he pushed back from the table. "Yeah, she does. He's sitting right here." If he was intimidated by Slim's thick frame, he definitely didn't show it.

"My bad, man. My bad." Slim and Heavy looked at each other and laughed. Up until now, they hadn't even acknowledged Bryce.

"Well, look here, bro, can you take our picture?" Heavy asked.

"Dude, we're trying to eat here," Bryce said, pointing to our plates.

"It's only gonna take a minute." Slim handed Bryce his phone. For a minute, I thought Bryce wasn't going to take it, but I flashed him a look to say, "just take it, please."

I stood, and both of the guys jumped on either side of me and put their arms around me. They cheesed hard as Bryce snapped the picture.

"A'ight, I need one by myself," Heavy said.

Bryce gritted his teeth, then tossed the phone on the table. They didn't seem fazed, because Slim picked the phone up and aimed it in our direction.

This time Heavy put both of his arms around my waist, like he was pulling me toward him. I tensed up, but he didn't seem to care, he was grinning so hard.

"Can you back up a little?" I said. "You're being real disrespectful to my friend."

"Sorry," Heavy replied. "Wouldn't want to make"—he turned to Bryce and smirked—"your friend mad."

As soon as he said that, I knew I'd messed up. Before I could say anything else, Slim snapped the picture, then said, "My turn, my turn."

If Bryce had been in a cartoon, he'd be having smoke come out of his ears right about now, so I knew we needed to hurry up with this little photo shoot.

Heavy held the camera up, and, just as he was about to snap, Slim leaned over real close, to the point that the sides of our faces were touching. I kept my smile when all I wanted to do was slap the mess out of him. I pushed him away when he tried to lean in and kiss me. "Dude, so not cool."

"Sorry, I just got a little carried away," he said, innocently.

"You 'bout to get carried up out of here," Bryce said, stepping toward them.

"Chill, man. Dang," Heavy said.

He snapped one more picture of me, then handed the phone back to Slim. "I mean, you are hanging out with a celebrity. A fine one at that, so you ought to be used to it."

Slim turned to me. "You need to check your boy. Let him know that when you're dating a celebrity, especially one that looks like you, he got to take what comes with the territory."

"Just go, please," I said.

"Cool." He took out a piece of paper and dropped it on the table in front of me. "But here's my number, just in case ol' boy ain't handlin' his business. I'll show you how a real man do it."

Bryce jumped up from the table. "Man, I'm a . . ."

Both of them took off, laughing.

I eased back down in my seat. "Can you believe the nerve of them?" I said, trying to force a laugh.

Bryce didn't see anything funny.

"What's wrong with you?" I asked.

"What do you think is wrong with me?" he snapped. "How you gon' just let them play me like that?"

"Play you like what? They were just taking some pictures."

"And you just grinning like you stuck on stupid while they disrespect your man."

I sighed. Was he really about to start trippin'?

"I told them to back up." I wasn't about to agree with Bryce and give him more reason to be mad.

"Yeah, but you kept taking the pictures." He glared at me, not bothering to hide his anger.

"Bryce, what was I supposed to do?"

"Tell them you were having dinner with your boyfriend!" he yelled. "Oh, sorry, apparently I'm not your boyfriend. I'm your *friend!*"

"Come on, just chill. It's not that serious." I tried to keep my voice even so he wouldn't get any more worked up. "I can't be going off on my fans. That's not a good look for my image."

"You know, I'm about sick of you and your image," he said, loudly enough for the couple at the next table to look our way.

"Shhhh," I said, putting a finger to my lips.

He huffed. "Excuse me," Bryce said, calling for our server. "Can we get our check please?" he asked as our waitress approached the table.

She set the check down on the table and scurried away like she was trying not to get caught in the middle of any drama.

"Really, Bryce?"

"Yeah, really," he said, opening his wallet and pulling out two one-hundred dollar bills. "I wish I had known we were just *friends*. Between the bracelet, this gift, this dinner, I've shelled out two grand. That's a lot of money for a *friend!*" He threw the money on the table. "Let's go." He headed out the door, not worrying about whether I was following him or not.

I hadn't meant for the friend comment to slip out. I seriously had meant nothing by it. Bryce was my man, and I wasn't ashamed of that. How had this evening turned out so badly?

Chapter 5

My fingers were starting to cramp. I knew I had to have signed over two hundred autographs. People had begun lining up here at the mall early this morning. I was helping with the grand opening of the new Miami Beach mall, and it seemed like it was going to be huge. The singer Miguel was performing, and I was signing autographs. At first, I wasn't feeling making an appearance at a mall opening. That stuff was reserved for beauty pageant queens. But the station had some kind of partnership with the mall and all but forced me to do it.

This creepy-looking guy approached the table. He had a 1980s jacket buttoned all the way up to his neck and some too-tight khakis. His long, stringy hair looked like it hadn't been washed in weeks, and even though I didn't smell anything, he looked like he stunk.

"C-can you sign my autograph?" he asked. He had my picture clutched closely to his chest.

Kennedi, who had tagged along for the event, stood behind me. She eyed him suspiciously, but I managed a smile and said, "Sure." I held out my hand to take the photo. "What's your name?"

"Ch-Chris," he stuttered.

"All right, Chris," I said, flashing another smile. *Smooches,* I wrote on my photo.

"Y-you're so beautiful," he said like he was in some kind of trance.

"Thank you very much, Chris."

I handed him his picture back. He lingered a bit too long before finally saying, "Thank you, I'm going to treasure it forever." He still didn't move; he just stood there staring at me like he was crazy.

I shot an evil look at Ariel, who was standing at the end of the table. She was supposed to be helping us to keep the line flowing, and she was just standing there looking stupid.

"I'm sorry, we have to keep the line moving," Ariel finally said. The strange guy reluctantly walked away, but he kept staring at me.

"Ewww," Kennedi said, leaning in and whispering to me. "Talk about creepy."

I laughed as I pushed her away. "Girl, be quiet and move." The line wasn't getting any shorter, so I needed to hurry up and make my way through these people.

I signed more autographs (the station had printed up tons of publicity photos), took a whole lot more pictures, then finally, the mall representative person said, "Okay, that's good."

I just then noticed that they'd cut the line off. Thank God. "Yes, I'm so ready."

"Me too," Kennedi echoed.

We gratefully followed the mall representative into a back room. I took a few more photos with mall staff, then ducked in the public restroom to use it.

"All set," my bodyguard, Mann, said.

"Yep," I replied.

"The girl who wants your job told me to tell you she was leaving." Kennedi laughed.

"Her name is Ariel." I chuckled.

Kennedi gave me a "whatever" shrug as we headed to the parking lot.

"You good?" Mann asked after he walked me to my car. "I can follow you home."

"Bye, Mann. I can make it from here." I smiled. I liked him a lot. Unfortunately, he was only with me at appearances and stuff. But Tamara was going to have to get with the program and hire him full-time for me soon. I bet Beyoncé never had to walk around without a bodyguard.

"Yeah, Mann," Kennedi leaned in and said. "If something happens, I'll protect her."

I laughed as Mann waved bye and watched me pull away. I had just turned out of the mall when I noticed my diamond promise ring from Bryce was missing.

"Oh no!" I said. "My ring."

"What about it?" Kennedi asked.

"I left it."

"Left it where?"

I thought for a minute. "I had to have left it in the restroom when I washed my hands."

"You should stop wearing that cheap jewelry, and you won't have to take it off before you get it in water," Kennedi joked as she leaned back and began playing with her phone.

"Ha, ha, you got jokes," I said, making a U-turn to go back into the mall.

"You want me to go with you?" Kennedi asked as I pulled up in front of the mall and double-parked.

"Nah. I'll be right back."

Kennedi turned up the music and started bobbing her head as I jumped out of the car.

I made my way back into the restroom, praying that my ring was still there. I breathed a sigh of relief when I saw it right where I had left it. I had just slipped it back on my finger when the door to the bathroom opened. I didn't pay it any attention until I looked up and saw the person who had just come in.

"This is a women's restroom," I said, instinctively backing up.

"I-I know. I s-saw you run in h-here, and I just had to see you again."

My heart started racing as Chris took a step toward me. "I was just sitting out there reading when I saw you." He pointed toward the door. "I think, it was, it was like some kind of divine intervention."

I looked at him like he was crazy but didn't say a word because homeboy looked like he wasn't wrapped too tight.

"It would m-make my day if I could just have a kiss," he stuttered.

"I don't think so," I said, stepping back again. "Get away from me." I tried to push past him, but he grabbed my arm.

"Why do you have to be so mean?" he snapped.

His tone caught me off guard, and my whole body tensed up. He no longer sounded like some creepy nerd. His voice was deeper, and he scowled like some kind of madman.

"I can't stand teases like you," he said, pushing me up against the wall.

"I was nice to you," I managed to say.

"But you're not being nice now. If you were nice to me, you would give me a kiss!"

"Okay," I said, trying to keep him calm. "I didn't mean anything by it; it's just that I don't kiss strangers."

"I bet you kiss your boyfriend, Bryce."

If I hadn't been scared before, I was definitely freaked out now. How did he know who my boyfriend was?

"Excuse me, but I really have to get going. My friend is waiting." I again tried to push past him. He grabbed me again and tried to force a kiss. Before I could scream, he put his hand over my mouth and pinned me harder.

"Let me go," I mumbled as his nasty hand covered my mouth.

I was just about to try and bite the mess out of him when the door to the bathroom swung open.

"What are you doing?" a girl screamed as she raced toward us. She took her purse and hit him over the head. "Let her go!"

The girl kept kicking and hitting him until he let me go. She grabbed my hand and pulled me toward the door. "Let's go!"

She didn't have to tell me twice. I raced out of the bathroom behind her and didn't stop until we were out among the crowds of people again.

I immediately began scanning the crowd for a security guard. "Are you okay?" she asked.

I tried to catch my breath. "Oh my God, I can't believe that."

"Did he hurt you?" she asked, examining me.

"No, no. I'm okay. Thank you so much. Who knows what he would've done." I felt myself fighting back tears. I took a moment to pull myself together. "I need to find a mall security guard."

"Are you going to be okay?" she asked again.

I nodded as I kept looking for a security guard. "Hey," I said, spotting one. "Excuse me, officer," I called out, waving toward him.

"Yes, ma'am, may I help you? Is something wrong?" he added when he noticed my panicked look.

"Come on," I told the girl who had helped me.

I turned, and the girl who had just literally saved my life was gone. Did she really leave without saying anything?

I shook my head. I couldn't worry about her. I quickly began explaining what had happened to the security guard, who didn't seem all that interested. I thought about tracking down the mall representative who had set up my appearance, but she'd have to tell my station, and Tamara would fuss about my sending Mann away when I had been the one begging for them to hire him in the first place.

No, I chalked this one up to my letting my guard down—something I vowed never to do again.

Chapter 6

I had just wrapped up another bomb taping and was absolutely worn out. I had also taken two tests and had three meetings today. Yeah, I couldn't wait until graduation, because this balancing act was killing me.

That's why Tamara's summoning me to her office on my way out the door was more than a drag. I was tired and meeting with Tamara was definitely not on my list of things I felt like doing right now.

Even still, I poked my head in her office door. "Hey, Tamara. You wanted to see me?"

She excitedly waved me in. I didn't sit down, because I didn't want her to think I was staying long.

"Great show today, Maya."

"Thanks," I said, looking at her like "I know that's not what you called me in here for."

"Well, you know at *Rumor Central*, we go digging."

"Yeah." I nodded as I tried to figure out where this conversation was going. Of course I knew that. I was the one doing most of the digging.

"So," Tamara continued, "we just had to figure out who

was the person responsible for making Maya Morgan a hot topic on social media."

I raised an eyebrow. "Yeah, me. I'm the one responsible."

Tamara laughed. "Besides you, of course. We know there would be no hot topic if it weren't for you. But someone was helping us trend each week. So, at your suggestion, we put those *Rumor Central* skills to work and found out who it was, and actually it was your own assistant who was able to dig up a name for us."

So, Ariel was good for something? She'd found the person behind the *Rumor Central* Twitter handle.

"Well?"

"It's the president of the Maya Morgan fan club."

"What fan club?"

Tamara leaned back in her chair. "The fan club that has over twenty thousand members."

Wow, I had a bona fide fan club. "That's what I'm talking about." I smiled.

"Kelly, can you send her in?" Tamara said into the intercom.

I waited in anticipation. How cool was this? I was actually about to meet the president of my fan club.

The door slowly eased open, and in walked a girl, with long, curly brown hair and deep dimples. She was dressed a little frumpily for my taste, but she looked like if you cleaned her up good, she could pass for Keke Palmer's twin sister. I studied her for a minute. She looked really familiar.

"Maya, this is Jayla Cooper," Tamara said.

"Hi, Maya." She was giddy with excitement. "It's a huge honor to meet you."

"Have we met before?" I asked.

She nodded. "It's an honor to meet you, officially. The last time we met was Saturday in a bathroom at the mall."

I jumped from my chair. "Oh, my, God. You're that girl

from the mall! The one who got that guy off of me in the restroom."

"What?" Tamara asked.

"Yeah, some creep followed me into the ladies' bathroom at the mall."

Tamara looked shocked. "What? Why didn't you say anything?"

"I don't know." I shrugged. I really had intended to say something, but it was my own fault that Mann wasn't around, and I didn't want anyone chewing me out for sending him away.

"What happened? Were you hurt? Where was Mann?" She started firing off questions.

"It's no biggie. Some guy followed me into the bathroom." A part of me wanted to tell the truth—that jerk had scared me to death, but I didn't need the drama, so I left it alone. I pointed at Jayla. "This is the girl that helped run the guy off. She beat him with her purse." I turned to face her. "Why didn't you introduce yourself then?"

"That wasn't the time or the place. I was actually there earlier to take some pictures for my blog site when I saw you go in the restroom. I was going to wait for you to come out and ask you a question."

"You have a blog site?"

"Actually, it's for you. It's called *All Things Maya*. We actually just got it up and running on Monday. I've been working on it a while. I sent you an email about it. But I know you're pretty busy." She was right. I got so many emails; no way could I reply to half of them.

"And Maya, this website is *phenomenal*," Tamara said, finally interjecting. "This girl right here is a technological genius."

"Have a seat," Tamara continued, speaking to Jayla. "This site has all the bells and whistles." Tamara motioned for me to come around her desk so I could see. I was amazed. It didn't look like a blog site. It looked like a bona fide website, designed by some expensive web designer. The colors were my favorite, pink and silver. The writing was classy. All the photos of me were my absolute best. This thing was off the chain.

"I just wanted to make it nice, because I'm like your biggest fan ever," Jayla said. "This is just for now. I'm actually working on something a little more high-tech."

"Something better than this?" I said.

She nodded modestly.

"Well, I love this, so I can only imagine how I'll feel about anything that looks better than this," I said.

She looked relieved to have gotten my approval.

"I still think you should've said something," I said to Jayla as I walked back around Tamara's desk.

"You weren't in any condition to meet anyone new," she replied. "Besides, I knew one day I'd get to meet you correctly."

"Well, we're looking forward to big things with Jayla," Tamara said. "I just wanted you to take a look at the site. If you like what you see, then we'd love to have her work with you to help you build your brand."

I looked at Jayla and smiled. "Well, I love it, and make sure we have your info." I looked back at Tamara. "Because I'm with the boss. We need to see how we can make you a permanent part of the *Rumor Central* team."

Jayla's eyes grew wide. "Wow, I'd like that. B-but . . ."

"But what?" Tamara asked. "Please don't tell me that's not something you'd be interested in. I think you'll be pleased with the terms."

"Oh, it's not that," she said. "I'd work for Maya for free. It's just, I'm eighteen. . . . I'm still in high school. I graduate in May, but I'm still in school."

Tamara and I laughed. "Around here at *Rumor Central*, age ain't nothing but a number," I said.

She broke out in a huge smile. "Then let me say I'd love to work for you, and I look forward to talking to you more."

"Give all your info to my secretary on your way out," Tamara said.

She nodded, rose and turned to leave. But she stopped and turned back to me. "Maya, let me just say, I can't wait to get to know you better."

"I second that, Jayla Cooper. Hope to see you soon."

"I love it," Tamara said after she was gone. "All this young talent."

"That's the best kind to have." I stood and headed to the door. "And I guess I need to thank Ariel."

Tamara nodded. "We both do, because I think this was a score for *Rumor Central*."

Chapter 7

I couldn't believe Bryce still hadn't called me. Usually, when he got mad, he cooled off after a couple of days, but so far, hadn't called me, and I wasn't about to pick up the phone and call him.

Even Sheridan noticed Bryce's stank attitude as we walked down the hallway on our way to lunch. Even though Sheridan and I had made up, I didn't share details about Bryce's and my relationship like I used to, so she didn't know what had happened between us.

"Girl, what is his problem?" Sheridan said when she saw Bryce side-eye me and keep moving.

I was dumbfounded that he was still trippin'. He had dropped me off at the house after dinner without saying a word to me. I had tried to talk to him on the way home, but he had just turned his music up louder.

"He's trippin' because he took me out and some guy fans wanted to take pictures."

Sheridan laughed. "He ought to be used to that by now."

I shrugged as I discreetly turned around to see if he really was going to walk off without saying a word to me. He was now at the end of the hall laughing and joking with his boys. Forget him. Two could play that game.

I turned back to Sheridan, ready to find the first guy I could to flirt with, when I saw Evian and Shay—my former *Miami Divas* costars—walking by us.

"What's up, Evian?" Sheridan said.

Evian turned her lips up and kept walking. She'd been upset with me since I outed her little cheerleading escort ring on my show. So while Sheridan and I had made up, Evian and Shay hadn't had two words to say to me.

They'd actually become distant from Sheridan as well. They'd told her if she was friends with me, she couldn't be friends with them. So junior high. Of course, Sheridan was like me; she didn't like anybody giving her ultimatums, so she basically told them where to go.

"I don't know why you keep speaking to them," I said.

Sheridan shrugged, unfazed as she kept tapping on her phone. "They'll get over it," she said.

"I don't care whether they do or not." But I did care about Bryce, and he was straight making me mad.

Sheridan caught me glaring back at Bryce again and took my arm, leading me away. "That's who you don't need to be letting see you mad. Whatever y'all arguing about, he'll get over it. But in the meantime, rule number one, never let your man see you fazed. Thirsty chicks are so not the business."

Sheridan was right. I followed her into the cafeteria without looking back.

We got our lunch trays, then sat down at our table, with our friends, Chasity and Ava. They weren't completely in our clique, but we did let them visit from time to time.

"What's up, Divas?" Ava said.

"Doing what we do," Sheridan replied.

"Being fabulous," I said, finishing her sentence.

Everyone laughed as we sat down and began eating. We talked about who was doing what with whom, whose girlfriend busted her boyfriend, who was flunking out and a bunch of other gossip, until finally, Chasity and Ava stood.

"It's been fun, but we gotta run," Chasity said.

"Yep, killer test next period," Ava added.

They waved goodbye and Sheridan and I finished up our meals.

"Hey, I talked to Valerie," Sheridan said as she pushed her empty tray away.

"How's she doing?" While I hoped that I never saw the psycho who'd tried to kill me last month, I did feel bad about how everything went down with her. She'd started working with me at *Rumor Central,* and, in some kind of whack attempt to be my friend, she'd shared a little secret about Sheridan—that Sheridan's mom had given up a baby for adoption to keep the pregnancy from hurting her career. Of course, what was I supposed to do with some good dirt like that? I aired it on *Rumor Central.* At the time, I didn't know that Valerie was the baby Sheridan's mom had given up. Needless to say, Valerie was livid. Her parents were furious, and she got into major trouble, including Sheridan's mom temporarily pulling her anonymous trust fund. Valerie tried to get revenge on me by stalking me to try and keep me from discovering her identity. Luckily, Sheridan stopped that lunatic just before she tried to kill me. Valerie's parents had moved away with her, but Sheridan was keeping in touch with her.

"She's okay," Sheridan replied. "I just think she and her parents are happy that my mom decided against taking away her money."

I took a final bite of my salad, then pushed my tray away as well. "Do you ever wonder if she would've been a geek if she'd grown up with you?"

Sheridan shrugged. "Not sure. It might've been kinda fun having a sister." She started playing with her leftover food, and I could see sadness all over her face.

I could tell she was getting down, and I had enough to

bring me down with the way Bryce was acting. So, I flashed a huge smile at her and said, "I'm still your sister."

She smiled back at me.

We talked about some more random stuff, then Sheridan said, "Oh, I forgot to tell you those were some cool pictures you uploaded to Instagram."

I shook my head. "Girl, I didn't have anything to do with that. That's all Jayla. She's been working for us for less than two weeks, and the girl has done more than the entire publicity team at *Rumor Central.*" The Instagram pictures Sheridan was talking about were some behind the scenes candid shots the station's photographer had taken the other day at Jayla's request.

Sheridan rolled her eyes. "That girl must have no life. All she does is sit up and promote you."

"It's her job now. And she likes it. Who am I to knock it? Plus, it's paying off. Her blog post got picked up by *Seventeen* magazine's website."

"Wow."

"So, say what you want about her, but Jayla is all right by me." I laughed.

By the end of the day, I was just all too ready to go home. I was glad to have the day off from the station, because I'd been working a grueling schedule, and today I was just going home to veg out in front of the TV.

Sheridan and I had just walked outside after school when I saw Jayla standing by my car.

"Jayla?" I said, surprised.

"Hi, Maya!" She grinned widely as she waved.

Sheridan didn't speak as she folded her arms and looked at Jayla like she was crazy.

Jayla came bouncing toward me. "I tried to call you."

"Yeah, I left my phone at home today." I was still trying to figure out what in the world she was doing at my school.

"Well, I just wanted to let you know about a few things I

had in the works, and I was getting you set up on Pinterest and I needed your passwords."

"What you need her password for?" Sheridan said, stepping to the side of me.

I laughed. "Down, girl. How is she going to update and upload my stuff if she doesn't know my password?"

Jayla just grinned at Sheridan, then handed me a piece of paper, and I wrote the password down. "But you really could've just called," I said as I handed the paper back to her.

"I tried. And we really need to get the photo gallery up and running."

"Well, you wasted a trip because I use the same password for almost everything," I said, pointing to the paper.

"It's not a wasted trip because, remember, I talked about getting photos of you at school. So I just want to get some pictures of you talking to your friends on campus."

I sighed. I so wanted to get home, but then I saw Bryce hanging out in front of the school with his boys.

"Cool. Let me put my bag in my car," I said. I tossed my bag in the backseat. "Good thing I'm looking on point."

Jayla grinned. "Oh, I wasn't worried about that. I knew you were always on point."

My hands went to my hips, and I tossed my hair over my shoulder diva-style. "See, I knew there was a reason I liked you."

She snapped a picture by my car, then we headed across campus—in the direction of where Bryce was standing. I wanted him to have a front-row seat to my photo shoot.

Sheridan followed, keeping her arms folded across her chest. We walked around, taking candid shots with Jayla's professional camera. I called Chasity and Ava over to get in some shots. Then a couple other of my friends. Of course, Bryce's boys came over, teasing me and flirting on the low-low. I put on a show, and, although Bryce was trying to act like he wasn't looking, I knew it was eating him up, especially when I asked several of his teammates to get in a picture. They all crowded around me, and the two teammates he couldn't stand got on both sides of me and hugged me while everyone else struck poses. That's when I saw Bryce storm off, and I couldn't help but smile.

After about twenty minutes, Jayla said, "Well, I'd better get going now. I want to get these uploaded tonight."

"Okay, see you later." I waved as she walked away.

"That girl creeps me out," Sheridan said once Jayla was gone.

"Everybody creeps you out," I replied.

"And she's so lame. Seriously, who gets all excited about picture taking and posting stuff about other people?" She shook her head like Jayla thoroughly disgusted her.

"She's a tech geek. Plus, I told you, we hired her at the station, so she's just doing her job. I'm not knocking her."

Sheridan stood watching Jayla as she pulled out of the school parking lot. "Unh-unh. It's just something about her. And I'm not feeling you giving her your passwords. Let her be your spokesperson or something and update your stuff for you, but don't just give her an all-access pass to your stuff."

"I don't have time to do all that stuff," I said, heading back to my car. "She is just going in and updating everything. It's no big deal."

"If you say so," Sheridan said.

I smiled. "I say so. I'm out. Don't call me, because my phone won't be back on. Today is all about me."

"When is it not all about you, Maya?" She laughed. "When is it not?"

Chapter 8

I have a boyfriend. Even if he's trippin', I have a boyfriend.

I had to keep telling myself that over and over. But the jacked-up part was I found myself wondering if I really *did* have a boyfriend. Bryce hadn't talked to me in over two weeks now. I was trying to be patient, but he ought to know, Maya Morgan didn't hold out for anyone.

And, judging from the way J. Love was all up in my face, I didn't have to.

"So, tell me again why a girl as fine as you doesn't have a man," he said, leaning in closer to me. J. Love was an R & B singer who had to be the hottest thing going right now. He was so fine, it was ridiculous. He had smooth chocolate skin, curly hair, and a body that was out of this world. He looked like a much finer version of Trey Songz.

I shook myself out of the trance his sexy voice seemed to be luring me into. It was no wonder he had passed Chris Brown as one of the top R & B singers. Between his looks and his voice, he was all of that. "I'm interviewing you," I said. "Not the other way around."

He grinned. "My mom always told me if you want to

know the answer to a question, just ask. So I'm asking." He grinned.

I couldn't help it; I crossed my long, Pilates-toned legs, making sure my thigh was peeking out from the slit in my pencil skirt. "Well, I don't know where you got the idea that I don't have a man."

He leaned back, disappointed. "Of course you do."

"I do." I paused. "Well, kinda, sorta. We're on the outs right now."

"In my book, that means no. So I need to know how I can get in."

I had to push down the butterflies turning backflips in my stomach. "Mr. Love . . ."

"J. For you, it's J," he said, cutting me off.

Oh, my, God! He was so fine!

"J," I said, pulling myself together. "I'm flattered, but—"

"Why don't you let me take you out?" He stared at me. Hard. Almost as if he were trying to put me into some kind of deep trance or something.

I wasn't about to let him intimidate me, so I stared right back. "Mr. Love, I don't mix business with pleasure."

He turned back to his publicist, who was standing off to the side. "Yo, Cheryl, is this interview over?"

She nodded. "It is. They only had fifteen minutes."

J. Love looked at his watch, which I had spotted right away was a Rolex Submariner. That watch was no joke. It cost $250,000. I knew because my mom had bought it for my dad for their anniversary, and he had made her take it back because it was "ridiculously expensive."

"It's been twenty minutes," J. Love said, looking up at me. "So it looks like you owe me five minutes."

I couldn't help but laugh. J. Love was so smooth. I had to give him his props. The cameraman who was taping the interview winked at me as he cut off his camera and walked off. J. Love stood and walked right in front of me.

"Seriously, our business is done. Let me take you out."

I was so tempted to say yes, but I really didn't want to do Bryce like that. Besides, there were a bunch of people standing around trying to act like they weren't listening, but I knew they were. I didn't want these busters all up in my business.

I stood, coming face-to-face with him. "I'm going to have to take a rain check, Mr. Love."

He put his hand over his heart. "I'm hurt." He reached in his pocket and pulled out a card. "But here's my private number. What time do you get off?"

"Actually, I'm done now." I took the card, although I had no plans to use it.

We stood for a minute, just staring at each other, and I felt my mind drifting to Bryce. A week and a half. Almost two weeks since I'd talked to him. What if he'd broken up with me and I let J. Love slip through my fingers.

"Let's at least go get something to eat," J. Love said. "I mean, my bodyguard will be there to protect me in case you try anything."

I laughed. "Oh, in case I try something? I don't think so."

"So, are you going to go or what? It's just dinner."

I knew a man like J. Love didn't have to beg anyone to go out with him, so I seriously was flattered. I checked my phone to see if Bryce had tried to call me while I was taping. He hadn't, and that made my decision for me.

"I guess I am a little hungry," I said.

J. Love chose a nice, quaint Italian restaurant on South Beach. The food was delicious, and the conversation was awesome. J. Love was so funny. He had me cracking up all evening, and by the time he dropped me back off at the station, I was so glad I'd decided to go with him. He tried to kiss me at the end of the night, but I stopped him. I liked him, but didn't want to give him the wrong idea. I had a reputation to protect, so I definitely couldn't get down like that.

Still, he called me the next day and asked me to come to the mall with him to help him pick out a gift for his mother. Since I didn't have anything to do for a change and couldn't pass up a trip to the mall, I told him to come pick me up.

We hadn't been at the mall ten minutes when I heard someone shout, "Oh my God, is that J. Love?"

"And Maya Morgan!" the girl who was with her shouted.

J. Love smiled and pulled me closer to him as people started snapping pictures. He was hugging all over me, and I immediately tensed up. That's all I needed was for my picture to show up on some blog for Bryce to see. Luckily, J. Love's bodyguard jumped in before too many more people could take pictures.

"If you don't mind, my man just wants to shop today," he said.

"Awww, I just want a quick picture," one girl whined. "Please. He's my favorite singer in the whole world."

J. Love nodded, and the girl jumped in between us.

"You two make such a cute couple," the girl said as she wiggled in the middle of us so her friend could snap the photo.

"We do make a cute couple," J. Love said after the girl had left and we'd resumed shopping. "Too bad you kinda sorta have a man." He smiled and took my hand and led me into the Gucci store.

"Where is everyone?" I asked once we were inside the store.

"I just wanted to shop in peace, so I had them close down for an hour."

"What?"

He shrugged like it was no big deal. Even I was impressed with that, and it took a lot to impress me.

The sales clerks stood off to the back, ready to serve if J. Love even acted like he was interested in something. I helped him find the most beautiful purse for his mother, then I picked up the flyest pair of Gucci shades I'd ever seen.

At the counter, I waited while the clerk rang J. Love up.

"Yo, throw those shades on there," he told the clerk, pushing the glasses toward her.

"Ummm, that's okay," I said, reaching to take them back. "I got it."

"Yo, ma, let me get the shades," he said, pushing my hand out of the way.

"I can buy my own shades."

He laughed. "I'm sure you can, but it's the least I can to thank you for helping me out. You sure you don't want anything else?" he asked. He motioned around the store. "Anything in here you want is yours, and I mean anything."

Now that was a dream come true. A super-rich dude giving me free rein to shop in the Gucci store! But I wasn't going out like that.

"No, I'm good. Just the glasses, and seriously, I can pay for them myself."

"Would you be quiet," he said, handing the clerk his black American Express card.

He handed me the glasses. "Thank you," I said with a wide grin.

"My pleasure. I just wish you'd let me buy you something else."

"I'm good."

He stared at me for a minute.

"What?" I said.

He shook his head and took my hand. "You're a girl after my own heart. Not one of the chicks I deal with would turn down a shopping spree in the Gucci store."

"Well, in case you haven't noticed, I'm not like all the other chicks you're used to dealing with."

"Oh, I've noticed, Maya Morgan. I've definitely noticed."

We laughed and joked the rest of the day. Thankfully, Darrell, his bodyguard, kept everyone at bay, so we shopped and enjoyed each other's company in peace. I could definitely see myself kicking it with him. But since I had a boyfriend, I had to settle for us being friends.

I actually was grateful to finally be heading home, since I was exhausted. I leaned back in the plush seat of his tricked-out Cadillac Escalade. J. Love was on the phone, wrapping up a call that had obviously stressed him out.

"Just get it handled, man," he said into the phone. "I can't afford this. Not right now." He ran his hand over his head. "So you got it taken care of? Cool. . . . I'll holla at you later."

"Everything okay?" I asked once he hung up. He seemed really intense.

"Yeah, my attorney just saved my behind," he replied, sounding relieved.

"What happened?" I shifted in the seat to get comfortable.

He hesitated like it had just dawned on him who he was talking to. "Let me be quiet since you're on that *Rumor Central* kick," he said.

"For your information, I'm off duty," I said. "And I don't mix *pleasure* with *business* either."

He smiled. "I like you, Maya Morgan."

"I like you, too, J. Love. So what's up? You seem really stressed."

He exhaled and leaned back in his seat. "Drama with my boys. Some of my crew invited these chicks out up in Seattle, and next thing you know, they were facing some sexual assault charges."

"What?"

"Oh, they didn't do it. But I can't have that kind of publicity. I just signed a major endorsement deal with Coca-Cola. Something like that could mess with my paper."

"Wow."

"Yeah, they even arrested me," he continued. "One of the girls tried to claim I was there. I wasn't even in the hotel." He shook his head like the memory made him mad. "That's why I always have to watch my back." He paused, looked at me like he was studying me. "I don't have to watch my back with you, Maya Morgan, do I?"

"Of course not," I said. And I meant that. I was really feeling J. Love, and I definitely wouldn't have sold him out. "So, how'd you keep it out of the press?" I asked.

"I have a good lawyer. I had to come up off a couple of grand, but it was worth it to shut this whole thing down."

"I'm glad to hear that," I said.

He turned to face me. "Really, Maya Morgan?"

"Yes, J. Love." I smiled.

"You know, you are a one-of-a-kind girl."

"I know." I snuggled up closer to him.

He hugged me. "And I'm going to do whatever it takes to make you mine. I got a feeling you'd be worth it."

I looked up at him. "I am."

He stared at me for a few minutes, then leaned in to kiss me. This time, I didn't stop him.

Chapter 9

"Bryce who?" That's all I could think as I sang along to J. Love's new track. He'd emailed me an MP3 file of the new song. It hadn't even been released yet, but he wanted my take on it. I knew within the first thirty seconds that this was about to be a hit.

After J. Love dropped me off last night, he called me, and we talked for his whole ride home. He invited me to his album-listening party next week. I gladly told him yes.

I knew it was early, but I was about to call Kennedi on ooVoo for a video chat and tell her that she was going to have to fly down so she could go with me. Sheridan and she would have to put aside any beefs, so all three of us could kick it.

I logged on and dialed my bestie's number. It took a minute, but finally the video of Kennedi filled the screen. She was still in bed.

"Hey Kennedi, it's Maya."

She poked her head from under the covers. "Whooaaa," I grimaced. "You look a hot mess."

She didn't find anything funny. "Are you doing drugs?" she asked.

"What?"

"You gotta be on something calling me at seven o'clock on a Sunday morning."

"You should be up going to church."

She yawned. "I am about to get my praise on at Church of my pillow and blanket."

"Well, wake up. I have something I needed to tell you."

She threw the covers back and stretched. "And you couldn't tell me at ten?"

"Nope. Guess who I spent the day with yesterday?"

"You and Bryce made up." She stretched and let out another long yawn. "Big deal. Like I didn't see that coming."

"Nope. It wasn't Bryce. It was J. Love."

She was quiet for a minute, then sat straight up in her bed. "J. Love, like Grammy-winning J. Love? Like make you wanna throw your thong on the stage, J. Love?"

"Yes, ma'am. *That* J. Love. I interviewed him earlier this week, then he took me out afterward."

Kennedi was wide-awake now. "And I'm just now hearing about this because . . . ?"

"Because you are always getting in trouble and got your phone taken," I replied. She'd sent out a group text to her friends to not send her any texts or call for three days because her parents had her phone.

"Well, I told you I was getting it back Friday. You could've called me then!"

"I'm calling now." Leave it to Kennedi to want the scoop as it happens. "Can you focus, please?"

"Okay, okay." She rubbed the sleep out of her eyes and leaned into the camera. "Tell me about this secret date."

"It wasn't secret," I said, getting comfortable myself. I stretched out on the chaise lounge in my oversized bedroom, adjusted my laptop, and continued telling her about my date. "We went to the mall. Girl, he shut down the Gucci store so we could shop."

"Are you freakin' kidding me?" she yelled. Oh, she was wide-awake now. "So what did you get?"

"He bought some stuff for his mom. I got a pair of glasses." I held up the Gucci shades so she could see them.

"Too cute. What else did you get?"

"That's it."

"What? J. Love is a multimillionaire, and all you got was a pair of glasses?"

I laughed because Kennedi was my girl, but she's that chick who would've cleaned the Gucci store out if J. Love had told her to get whatever she wanted. The funny part is she could've bought whatever she wanted out of there with her own money, but there was something about spending some guy's money that she loved.

"I only got the shades, because I'm not trying to use the boy like that. And I didn't want him to pay for those. I was going to get them myself, but he insisted. Then, he wanted to buy me some more stuff."

"And you didn't let him? Lord, where did I go wrong with my bestie," she wailed.

"Shut up, Kennedi. You know I'm not a gold digger."

"That's not gold digging. You're rich just like him. Well, maybe not just like him because, really, it's your dad who's rich, not you. But J. Love's money is his own."

"Kennedi—"

"My point is, a gold digger goes looking for rich dudes. I keep trying to tell you, that's not us. Rich dudes find us, and it's our responsibility to relieve them of their money and save our own." She was serious as a heart attack, too.

"Girl, you are so stupid. Anyway, after we left the mall, he dropped me off, and we talked all night. He said he felt an instant connection to me. Girl, he even opened up and told me about some legal drama he was going through."

"What kind of drama?"

I thought about not saying anything, but Kennedi was my

girl. If there was one person I could trust to never say anything, she was that person. "Well, apparently he got arrested in Seattle or something. His boys got with some groupies, and the girls claimed they were raped. Tried to involve J. Love and everything. But he wasn't even there."

"Dang, but I can imagine he always got some kind of drama going on."

"But I just love the fact that he trusted me enough to share that with me." Just talking about J. Love was giving me butterflies all over again.

Kennedi leaned across her bed. "That is so totally cool. How old is he?"

"He's twenty-one."

"Oh, my, God. Your mom is going to kill you."

"That's only, like, four years older than me."

"Okay, tell that to your mom. Does he know how old you are?"

"He didn't ask, but he knows I'm a senior in high school."

"Well, if he ain't trippin', I ain't trippin'." She laughed.

"Anyway, J. Love invited me to his album listening party next weekend, so you have to come down."

"Oh, you know I am so there," she said excitedly, before adding, "So, what does this mean for Bryce?"

"Bryce hasn't bothered to call me, so it means Bryce . . ."

". . . Is officially history," she said, finishing my sentence.

I chuckled, but I felt a twinge in my heart. "Maybe we're just taking a break for a minute, and I'm testing the waters."

"You know Bryce is all that, but he's like you, spending daddy's money. So, I say give J. Love a shot. Shoot, you guys could be some kind of power couple, like Beyoncé and Jay-Z."

"You're sure right about that." I glanced at the clock. "Okay, go back to sleep. I have to do some research for this story I'm working on. I didn't get anything done yesterday."

"You have me wide-awake now."

"Well, go back to sleep."

"Ugh, fine. Bye."

I hung up the phone. I was sure she'd be back out in no time, but me, on the other hand, I was too excited to sleep. But I really needed to focus. I had an interview tomorrow with the stars from *Twilight,* and I hated to admit that I hadn't seen any of the movies in the series. I just wasn't into vampires like that. But the one thing Tamara made clear, when it came to the entertainment portion of my show, I needed to know what I was talking about. And that meant watching their movies. So they'd sent me over a copy of *Twilight* 732, or whatever number they were on now, and so I needed to get to watching.

I popped the video in and got comfortable on my sofa. I don't know how much time had passed, but the next thing I knew, my mom was tapping me on my shoulder, and the credits were rolling.

"Maya, what are you doing?"

"Hey, Mom," I said, stretching. "I guess I fell asleep watching this movie."

"Since when did you get into vampires?"

"I'm not. It's some research I have to do for the show."

She walked over and turned the TV off. "Well, I've been meaning to talk to you. I got a progress report from your chemistry teacher."

I groaned. As much as I loved the new age, I wish we could go back to the days when they sent stuff in the mail and you had a chance to get it and hide it before your parents saw it. "Mom, I'm going to pull the grade up."

She looked at me sternly. "You'd better, because I told you, the only way I'm supporting this TV show thing is if you keep your grades up at school, and from the looks of things, you're not doing a very good job."

"I'm working on it, Mom," I said.

"Maya, if you flunk this class, your teacher said there's a chance you might not graduate."

"She's just being dramatic."

"Maya, don't play me for a fool, okay?" my mother said.

"I told you, it's not that serious. I'm going to do well in that class." That was a bold-faced lie. I didn't know how I was going to pass that class. Since Valerie had left, I hadn't had much help acing this class.

"You'd better," my mother warned. "If you want to keep digging up dirt, you'd better."

I let out a long sigh. Between this class, calculus, and a stupid English informative research paper I had to do—and I had no idea what I was going to do that paper on—I was slowly sinking into a big hole as far as school was concerned. I needed to figure out something and figure it out fast.

Chapter 10

My mom was right, I thought as I looked at the computer screen. An F on my chemistry exam would completely screw me.

My phone rang, and I logged off the website where we checked our grades. I didn't want to chance my mom popping back into my room and seeing that I was also failing calculus.

"Hey, Jayla," I said.

"Hey, Maya. I was just seeing if you had had a chance to look at the Pinterest page?"

"No, not yet. But I trust you, though," I said. "You've been doing an awesome job."

"Well, I like doing this stuff. I'm about to get back to work on the website."

"Do you ever do anything for fun?" I asked. "Because every time I talk to you, you're working."

She laughed. "This is fun to me. I actually like working."

I wanted to tell her I loved my job, too, but geesh, I did have a life outside of work. But since I needed her, I kept my mouth closed.

"Okay, well, I'll check it out. I won't be able to do it

today. I need to study for this stupid chemistry test. I hate this class." I blew a frustrated breath.

"Oh, you're not doing well in it?"

"No." I paused. "You wouldn't be any good at chemistry, would you?" I wasn't trying to get a tutor or anything, but I definitely could use someone to just do my work for me. It's not like I'd ever actually use chemistry again.

She chuckled. "Hardly. I'm good at techy stuff. But I hate chemistry." She hesitated again. "But . . . I am good at grade changing."

"What?" She had my full attention now.

"Well," she said, slowly, "this is just between you and me, but . . ."

"Will you say it already?" I said when she stopped talking.

"At my old school, right before the grading period ended, I would go in and change the grades right before the report cards printed," she admitted.

"Change the grades? How? How in the world are you getting into the school's system?" I didn't know how that was even possible. She might've been able to get away with that at her bootleg public school, but I definitely didn't see her being able to do it at Miami High. We had state-of-the-art everything, and I'm sure that included security systems.

"You said it yourself, I'm a technological genius."

"Ummm, well, you know the system at my school is top-notch."

"Never met a system I couldn't crack," she said.

I leaned back in my chair and considered what she was saying. Could I actually let her change my grade? I thought about that F and how I really didn't have time to study. Of course, I could.

"Wow, you mean, I wouldn't have to sweat chemistry, and I could still get an A?" I finally asked.

"I would probably shoot for a B. You don't want your mom getting suspicious."

"Good looking out. I might just have to take you up on that offer."

"Okay, just let me know."

I hung up the phone in awe. When it came to computers, was there anything that Jayla Cooper didn't know how to do? That girl was a beast. I was just glad to have her on my team.

Chapter 11

I was floating on cloud nine. I'd finally made my way through the *Twilight* series, so I was prepared for my interview. Now that I knew Jayla could fix my grade, I wasn't stressing over that chemistry test anymore. And J. Love had taken me out to see comedian Mike Epps last night, so yesterday had been a good day.

Now, I could focus on my show before dinner with J. Love again tonight. He was trying to squeeze in as much time with me as possible before he hit the road. Even though he'd be back for his party this weekend, he made no secret about how much he was feeling me and how he wanted to spend as much time with me as possible. I was loving every minute of it.

My assistant, Ariel, poked her head in my office. "Hey, are you ready?" she asked. "They're ready for you on the set."

"Cool." I grabbed my scripts and headed out to the studio. While I'd prepared for the *Twilight* interview, I was mostly excited about today's main gossip story. One of the stars of *Basketball Wives Miami* was creepin' with a married movie star, and she and the wife had gotten into a big fistfight, and both women had been arrested. They'd managed to keep it out of the news, but they couldn't keep it from me. I was about to blow their story up. I probably should've felt bad, but I didn't. I was no longer selling out my friends. I didn't know these chicks, so, oh well.

I headed onto the set, did my thing, then called it a day. I was ready to see what J. Love had in store for us this evening. He was leaving in the morning to go perform in Dallas and wanted to do "something special" before he left.

"Hey, Maya. Can I talk to you for a minute?" Tamara said on her way to her office.

I wanted to protest, because I was trying to get out of there since it was already seven o'clock, but I followed her anyway.

"Hey, Jayla," I said, when I noticed Jayla sitting in front of Tamara's desk. "You're working late."

"Oh, it's not that late," Jayla said.

"Sit, sit," Tamara said.

"I have somewhere I need to be."

"This will just take a minute." She smiled in Jayla's direction. "I was just complimenting Jayla because she, well, I'll let her tell you."

Jayla turned toward me, her face lit up with excitement.

"Well, today, the fan club hit our two hundred thousandth member."

"Wow," I replied, taking a seat. "We were just at twenty thousand people a few weeks ago."

"Yeah, that was before Jayla worked her magic," Tamara said.

"Dang," I said. I definitely had to give Jayla her props. This girl was off the chain.

"How did you do it?" I asked. I mean, I know I was the real reason for the boost, but she still had to have done something.

"Well, we've been trending a lot. That sparks interest in the Maya Morgan brand and that gets people talking and gets them over to all your social media pages. I made it easy to join the fan club by just clicking a tab on each page."

"I do have a question, though," I said. "If you build all these people on social media, what happens to the actual *Rumor Central* website?"

"Oh, that's the beauty of it all," Tamara said. "It all goes hand in hand. It's all about driving traffic from one site to the other."

"Yeah, we don't want to leave everything in Facebook, Instagram or Twitter's hands, because if they shut down, then what?" Jayla added.

"That's right," Tamara chimed in. "Jayla showed us why we want all roads to lead right back to *Rumor Central.*" She looked at Jayla in admiration.

I had to agree with Tamara. I didn't know where Jayla had come from. I was just glad that she'd come, because with her touch, my fabulous life would never be the same.

Chapter 12

My eyes had to be playing tricks on me. I stood in the middle of the hallway, mouth open. I wasn't the only one shocked. Sheridan, Chastity and Ava, had all stopped midsentence when they saw what I was looking at.

"Hey, Maya," Jayla said, bouncing over to us.

"Jayla, what are you doing here?" I asked. "It's the middle of the day. Why aren't you at school?"

"I'm at school." She grinned widely. "I'm a student here."

"Since when?" I balked.

"Since yesterday. I transferred here." She said that like it was no big deal.

"Excuse me? What do you mean you transferred?" I looked at her in disbelief. What kind of person just up and transferred in the middle of the semester?

"Who is this?" my friend Ava said.

Sheridan was the one who answered. "She works for Maya."

"So now your staff has to go to school with you?" Chastity asked.

I was too dumbfounded to even respond. I couldn't believe this.

Sheridan stepped closer to her. "Are you following my girl?"

"Oh, no, it's not even like that," Jayla protested, trying to keep a smile on her face. "I don't know if you'd heard, but they found asbestos at my school, and they had to move all the students. They allowed some of us to choose any school in the area. I was already in the midst of transferring when I met you," she said to me.

"I didn't even know they let people transfer in to Miami High," Chastity said.

"They only do that with scholarship students and people who are stupid rich," Ava said. Her eyes made their way up and down Jayla's body. "And I doubt that she would be in the stupid-rich category," Ava added with her nose turned up.

Jayla didn't seem fazed. I had to shake myself out of my stunned trance.

"That's just really convenient, isn't it?" Sheridan said, her arms folded across her chest.

"Okay, I'm sorry, I'm a little confused here," I said. "Why didn't you mention that you were transferring?"

"I didn't see why it mattered," Jayla said.

Was she serious? "You didn't see how it mattered?" I repeated. My girls were standing on both of my sides. I know we looked like we were ganging up on Jayla, but she needed to give me some answers.

"What's the big deal?" Jayla asked.

"The big deal is she doesn't like obsessive freaks following her around," Sheridan snapped.

Jayla put both hands on her hips. If Sheridan was scaring her, she didn't show it.

"I'm not a freak, and I'm not obsessive. I'm just good at my job. And my transferring here didn't have anything to do with Maya. But if anything, I'd think she'd be happy."

I couldn't understand why Jayla hadn't mentioned that she was transferring before. But her being here wasn't the only thing that had my mouth on the floor. It was what Jayla was wearing.

"Like, ewww," Chastity said, just now noticing her outfit. "Are you seriously wearing a T-shirt with Maya's face on it?"

"Yeah." Jayla looked down at her shirt, pulling it out for everyone to see. "I had them made. We give them away to Maya's fans. Would you guys like one?"

"As if." They burst out laughing.

"Yeah, I'm good," Ava said.

"Ummm, I'll pass, too," Chastity added.

I wanted to laugh because they were like me. They wouldn't be caught dead wearing a celebrity's T-shirt, especially if that celebrity was someone you knew. That was lame with a capital *L*.

"Okay, okay, just chill," I said, jumping in before they started drawing attention. "So you transferred here," I said turning back to Jayla. "That's cool, but ummm, the shirt? So not feeling it."

She actually looked hurt. "You don't like the shirt?"

"What do you think, genius?" Ava snapped. I held out my hand to quiet her.

"No, I love the shirt," I told her. "I really do. It's just something about having you wear it around school. Let's just not."

She hesitated. It was obvious she was disappointed. "Okay, I won't wear it again," she finally said. She pulled a jacket out of her bag. "I'll just put my jacket on over it."

All of us stood and watched as Jayla put the jacket on and zipped it up.

"Much better," I said.

She stood there awkwardly for a minute, then finally said, "Well, I'm not trying to get in your way or anything. In fact, my best friend goes here; that's the real reason I chose this school. So that's where I was headed, to meet her."

"Who is your best friend?" Sheridan said, like she didn't believe her.

"Maggie Long."

"Who is that?" Ava asked.

"Is that that scholarship girl, the freshman?" Chastity said.

"Yeah," Jayla replied. "That's her."

"Your best friend is a freshman?" Ava asked, not bothering to hide her disgust.

Jayla nodded. "Yeah, and?"

Chastity coughed and muttered, "Loser," under her breath.

"I'm gonna leave you guys alone," Jayla said, sounding all sad. "Sorry, Maya, if I freaked you out. I thought you'd be cool with it."

I gave her a tight smile as she walked off.

"And the freak of the week award goes to Maya's new publicist," Chastity said after Jayla rounded the corner.

"She's not my publicist," I protested. "She just does my social media stuff."

"She's your number one fan," Ava sang.

They laughed some more before Sheridan finally said, "Seriously, Maya, you don't see anything creepy about this?"

I shrugged. "She may be a little strange, but I can't help it that she thinks I'm fabulous and you guys don't recognize all this fabulosity." I did a little twirl. I was trying to lighten the mood, but I was serious, too.

"Oh, my, God. What were we thinking," Sheridan said in a high-pitched fake voice.

Chastity pretended to clutch her pearls. "We are so sorry, Your Highness. I mean, can we pretty please get some T-shirts of you so that we can walk around with your face on our boobs? Pretty please?"

Ava clasped her hands together excitedly. "And while we're at it, we should get some sweatbands, headbands, and glasses that say Maya Morgan."

"Ooooh, great idea," Sheridan said. She pointed to her behind. "And I'm going to get 'Maya' on this butt cheek, then 'Morgan' on this butt cheek."

They cracked up laughing again. I couldn't help but laugh, too. "You guys are so stupid."

We laughed for a minute as we made our way down the hall to our classes. Ava and Chastity went on their way. Sheridan stopped me just as I was about to go into my class.

"Seriously, Maya. I'm not feeling Jayla. You don't think it's weird that she just so happened to be transferring to your school?"

"She's harmless." As soon as I said it, I realized I had said that exact same thing about Valerie, and look at how that ended, with her trying to kill me at my father's cabin. "Nah," I said, "Jayla is harmless. A little freaky, but harmless, nonetheless."

Chapter 13

I made my way into my office and had just taken the top off my Fiji water when I looked up to see Ariel standing in my doorway. She didn't have her usual smile on and was instead staring at me like she wanted to wring my neck or something.

"May I help you?" I asked.

She still didn't say anything and just kept glaring.

"What in the world is your problem?" I said.

She walked into my office like she'd received a personal Evite. "People like you," she snarled.

My mouth fell open. "Excuse me?"

"You know, it's so unfair how people like you come up. Everything is just laid out for you on a silver platter, so you don't know what it's like to work hard."

This trick had lost her mind. As hard as I worked trying to balance school and stay on top of my job here at *Rumor Central*, she had me messed up.

She continued. "You were lucky enough to be born into money, so you think you're better than everyone else."

"Ariel, what in the world are you talking about? Have

you completely lost your mind? Did you forget who you work for?"

She folded her arms defiantly. I swear, if I didn't know better, I'd think she had a split personality and this was the crazy one. I'd never seen her act like this. "Oh, trust. I didn't forget who I work for. You won't let me forget that I work for you."

"It is what it is. That's the whole reason you're here—to be my assistant. If you have a problem with that, there's the door." I pointed to the door she'd just walked through.

She just glared at me. "You know, if you didn't want to help me, all you had to do was say you didn't."

"You know what, get out of my office," I said, turning around in my seat and dismissing her. "I'm tired. I don't have time for your drama."

She walked over and had the nerve to slam her demo tape down on my desk. "Juan from maintenance gave me my tape. He found it in the trash."

Oops. I almost said, "And?" But I just shrugged and said, "I was looking for it. I didn't know what had happened to it. It must've fallen off my desk and into the trash can."

"You are such a liar."

"And you are so out of line," I said slowly. "I know you're older than me, but remember who's still the boss."

"All I wanted was your help."

"Why don't you do the job that we pay you to do," I said. "Then we can worry about all that other stuff later. Besides, you really should be somewhere at least a month before you start trying to take someone else's job."

"So, is that what you're worried about, my taking your job?"

I had to laugh at that. "Honey Boo Boo, please. In your wildest fantasy, you couldn't take anything from me. In fact the only thing you need to be taking is notes."

"I'm majoring in radio, TV, film," she said, like that was supposed to mean something.

"And while they're teaching you in the classroom, I'm working it in the studio as one of the hottest hosts in the country. So if you had any common sense, you'd be trying to soak up all the knowledge you could from me."

She just kept glaring, looking like she'd give anything to punch me in my throat. I didn't know what in the world was her problem, but she was definitely pushing me.

"Now, I'm going to understand that you're emotional and give you a pass on this little outburst," I continued, pointing my finger at her. "But don't ever come at me like that again."

"So, I guess this means you won't help me get on air?"

"You guessed right."

She nodded as she bit her bottom lip, like she was trying to calm herself down. "As long as I know where I stand."

"Yeah, so now you know. Now, beat it." Under normal circumstances, I wouldn't have been as mad, but she had lost her dang mind coming in my office calling me a liar. This was exactly what I was talking about. Hate was coming at me from every direction.

My sour mood was immediately erased when my phone rang and I looked at the caller ID. Seeing J. Love's number immediately put a smile back on my face and wiped away any anger.

"Hello," I sang.

"Hey, beautiful, whatcha doing?"

"Just wrapped up on set. You?"

"Same thing. Just finished sound check and now chillin' before the show. You having a good day?"

"Yeah, just had a little tiff with my assistant. You know I'm always catching it because of my age. Folks think they can step to me any kind of way."

"Hope you handled her."

"You know I did."

We held the phone for a minute, then he said, "You miss me?"

"I sure do. When will you be back?"

"In three days, just in time for my party. Sorry I haven't been calling like I wanted. It's just been really grueling out here. Doing a different city every night, then promotions all day long."

"Nah, it's cool. You know I know how it goes."

"See, that's what I'm talking about. And you don't trip about my schedule."

"A confident girl never trips over something like that."

"You know what, Maya Morgan? I don't know about your kinda sorta man, but I'm not gonna rest until I make you my girl."

"We'll see, J. Love. We will see." I had to play that role, but J. Love just didn't know that was music to my ears.

Chapter 14

School should really be optional. That's all I could think as I glanced out the window, wishing I could be anywhere but in this boring English class. Mrs. Williams, my English teacher, was talking some "Where forth art thou" mess. Again, useless information.

I wasn't the only one who was ready for this class to end, because when the bell rang, everybody jumped up so fast you would've thought the place was on fire.

"Don't forget to start on those research papers," Mrs. Williams called out as we raced toward the door. "You will have to orally present them in front of all the classes. Those are thirty percent of your grades, and I don't want to hear any excuses."

I didn't want to hear anything about a research paper. I hadn't thought twice about that thing, even though I knew I needed to get started. It was supposed to be an informative paper, from which our classmates could learn some valuable information. We were making our presentations in a few weeks, and I still had no idea what I was doing.

I saw Jayla heading into the class, which she had after me. I was just going to see if she could find me a topic to write about, then I'd make Ariel do all the research. Ariel might be mad now, but if she valued her job, she'd quickly get over it.

"Jayla," I called out. She actually kept walking.

What the . . . ? I spun around and went in the classroom after her. "Jayla, did you hear me call you?" I asked as she took a seat in the back of the room.

She looked up from her seat, and I couldn't make out the look in her eyes, but it was almost like she had an attitude with me.

"Did you hear me?" I said.

She paused, then said, "Sorry, my mind was somewhere else."

The whole way she said it was cold. "What's wrong with you?" I asked.

She just glared at me before saying, "Nothing."

"Obviously something is, since you're acting like I peed in your punch or something."

She shrugged. "Nah, I'm good."

I looked over my shoulder to make sure Mrs. Williams wasn't listening. "Have you come up with the topic for your research paper yet?"

"No. Why?"

"Because when you do, I was hoping you could find me a topic too."

Again, she didn't say anything, just sat there staring at me.

"Is that going to be a problem?" I asked.

She shrugged again. "Nah, it's cool. Anything for the great Maya Morgan."

My hands went to my hips. "What is that supposed to mean?"

Before she could answer Bryce walked in, laughing, his arm around this girl named Callie. As soon as he saw me, he lost his smile. So did Callie. She quickly pulled away from him.

"M-Maya, I'm sorry, I . . ."

Bryce cut her off. "Nothing to be sorry about. Maya and I aren't together anymore."

I couldn't help but let out a little snortle. Glad to know it was official now.

"Yeah, I've moved on," I said.

"Oh, yeah," some Valley Girl sitting in the row next to Jayla said. "You're dating the singer, J. Love, right?"

I grinned. "Yeah, we're together now." Okay, I was exaggerating, but the way Bryce was gritting his teeth, the lie was well worth it.

"Oh, my, God. He is sooo fine," the girl said.

"And isn't he like stupid rich?" the girl sitting next to her asked.

"That he is." I looked at Callie. "So, don't let me stop you." I looked Bryce up and down. "I've moved on to bigger, better, finer, and *richer* things."

With that, I spun and walked out of the room.

Chapter 15

Tonight was the night. J. Love's party. He'd been out of town all week, but he was supposed to get back this afternoon. I was a little shocked that I hadn't heard from him today. But I did know that he had back-to-back tours, so I gave him a pass.

"Girl, I cannot wait." Kennedi interrupted my thoughts as she swirled around in her dress. We'd spent all evening in the mall, trying to get ready for the party tonight.

"I can't believe we are actually going to party with J. Love," Kennedi said.

"Shhhh," I said. "Keep your voice down. I don't want my mom trippin' about us going to an industry party."

Kennedi stopped and modeled in front of my full-length mirror.

"Doesn't she know that you're a celebrity?"

"Yeah, tell me about it." I pushed my diamond hoop earrings through my ears. "But she's still on that 'you're still underage, and as long as you're under my roof, you'll do as I say' routine."

"Man, that sucks," Kennedi said.

I handed her backpack to her. "So take that dress off and just put your stuff in here. We're going to get dressed at Sheridan's house."

She took the backpack and began stuffing her six-inch heels and makeup bag into it.

She slipped her dress off and put it in the bag, too. "I still don't understand why Sheridan has to go," she said, slipping on some jeans and a T-shirt.

I took a deep breath. "We have been through this a thousand times. You two are just going to have to learn to get along, because neither one of you is going anywhere."

"Yeah, but she stabbed you in your back by trying to get with Bryce. You act like you've forgotten that, but I haven't."

"*And?* You stole Kevin's iPod and blamed it on me."

"That was in the sixth grade!" Kennedi protested.

"Whatever, the point is, I forgave you. So chill with all the negativity." I went back to packing, taking care as I folded my coral sequined minidress and placed it in my bag. I had to make sure I was on point tonight. I had asked J. Love how many of his women would be there tonight, and he had assured me that I would be the only one who mattered.

"Fine, fine," Kennedi said. "I'm going to have a good time regardless. It's about to be on and poppin'," she said, doing a little dance.

I sent my mom a text to let her know that we were leaving, then we quietly made our way out the back door. Twenty minutes later, we were pulling up to Sheridan's massive seven-bedroom house.

"Hey, Kennedi," Sheridan said dryly when she answered the door.

Kennedi just raised an eyebrow, but didn't speak.

"Look, you two," I said, "I'm gonna leave both of your stank behinds here and go to the party by myself if you can't learn to get along."

"Okay, fine," Sheridan said, then she did a big, fake, cheesy grin. "Helll-llloo, Kennedi. It's such a pleasure to see you!" she said in a fake excited voice.

"And you, too, dah-ling," Kennedi replied as they air-kissed.

"Okay, now you guys are going overboard." I brushed both of them aside as I walked inside Sheridan's house. "Let's go get dressed. I want to be fashionably late, but not too late."

We went into Sheridan's room and got dressed. We listened to music as we laughed, joked, and teased each other. It felt really good to have my two best friends getting along for a change. I guess the party had us all psyched, so no one was interested in causing any drama tonight.

We took Sheridan's Benz and, an hour later, were sitting in front of the club where J. Love was holding his party.

"Wow, look at that line," Kennedi said as we pulled up to the valet.

"Ugh, I hope we're not waiting in that, because Sheridan Matthews does not do lines." Sheridan shook her head like she'd rather turn around and go home before standing in line.

"Girl, please," I replied. "You know I'm not waiting in nobody's line." I sashayed to the front of the line.

"Where they think they're going?" some girl yelled.

"Get to the back of the line," someone else shouted.

It was Kennedi who turned around and said to the second girl in her Chris Brown voice, "Why you hatin' from outside the club? You can't even get in."

We all busted out laughing.

"We were here first. We've been waiting forever," the girl next to her shouted. She had on a super-short miniskirt and a tank top. Both her friend and her had on cheap patent leather heels, so I know their feet had to be killing them.

"And you're *still* going to be waiting," Sheridan told her.

"Yep, wait out here with the other riffraff." Kennedi laughed.

"I got your riffraff," the girl in the miniskirt said.

"You just tagging along anyway," her friend chimed in.

"Whatever, loser," Kennedi said. "Gimme your number. I'll text you and tell you how the party is inside."

Sheridan and she high-fived each other. I shook my head and turned my attention to the bouncer.

"Hi, I'm Maya Morgan. I should be on the VIP list," I said, pointing to his clipboard.

He scanned the list. "Umm, I don't see your name."

"Well, then you need to look again. I'm sure it's there," I said confidently.

He glanced down, then back up. "I'm sure it's not."

"I was personally invited by J. Love."

He narrowed his eyes at me and looked at me like I was lying. "Your name isn't on the list. Get to the back of the line."

Oh, he was trippin' for real. Sheridan and Kennedi were no longer laughing and had moved in closer to me to see what was going on.

"Umm, I'm sorry, do you know who I am?" I said.

"Umm, I'm sorry, do you know I don't care who you are? You're not on the list, so get to the back of the line."

The girls who Kennedi and Sheridan had gotten into it with were eating this up. One of them had actually pulled out her phone and started recording us.

Kennedi leaned over to me. "What's going on, Maya?" she whispered.

"Just chill," I said. "I'm sorry." I flashed a smile at the bouncer. He was about seven-feet tall, so my getting an attitude would get us nowhere. I needed to pull out the charm. "I'm Maya Morgan, the host of *Rumor Central*."

"Well, I'm Tank, the bouncer, and your name *still* isn't on the list," he said in a gruff voice.

"You don't understand," I said, slowly losing confidence, "J. Love and I are . . . special friends."

"Oh, I understand. You're just like every other chicken head out here claiming to know J. Love so you can skip to the front of the line."

Did this fool just call me a chicken head??? Oh, I was so going to have his job.

"This is ridiculous," I said, pulling out my phone. I called J. Love, and it went straight to his voice mail. I hung up and scrolled through until I found his assistant's number.

"Hey, Kimmie, this is Maya Morgan," I said when she answered. I could hear lots of noise and music, which meant she was inside the club. "I'm at the front door. Can you come tell them to let me in? The bouncer is saying my name isn't on the VIP list, and I can't get in."

Kimmie was quiet for a minute. "Hello, Kimmie?"

"Yeah, Maya," she finally said. "Ummm, your name *isn't* on the list."

"Excuse me?"

She paused, then continued. "It's not on the list. I'm sorry."

"Kimmie, what in the world is going on?"

Just then, the crowd screamed as J. Love rolled up in his limo.

"Un-unh, J. Love is here. I'm going to talk to him and find out what is going on." I hung up before she could say anything else.

Kennedi and Sheridan followed me over to the limo.

I could tell Kennedi and Sheridan were embarrassed. Shoot, so was I. I'd never been more embarrassed in my life.

I pushed my way to the front. Darrell, J. Love's bodyguard, immediately stepped in front of me to stop me.

"Wha . . . ?" I asked, stunned as I flinched at his hand blocking me.

He didn't say anything as he stood staring at me.

"Seriously, Darrell?"

Darrell looked back at J. Love, who nodded, so the burly bodyguard stepped aside and let me pass.

I cut my eyes at him as I walked over to J. "Hey, what's up? You invite me to this party, and my name isn't even on the list to get in."

J. Love actually turned his nose up at me. "Yo, shawty, if it ain't on the list, it ain't on the list." He was so cold to me; it was crazy. This couldn't be the same guy who just a few days ago had been vowing to make me his girl.

"Excuse me?" I said in shock. "J, what's going on?"

"Look here, shawty," he said stepping toward me. So now I was "shawty"???? "You cool and all, and I was looking forward to kickin' it with you, but I don't do backstabbers. And I especially can't stand chicks who try to run game."

"What are you talking about?"

He looked at me, and I couldn't be sure, but it almost looked like I saw hurt on his face.

"I'm talking about the story."

"What story? I haven't done a story on you. I *wouldn't* do a story on you."

"Yeah, but you'll sell me out. Just like every other gold-digging chick in my life. How much did they pay you? Did you do it so you could get some shine?"

"J, what are you talking about?"

"He's talking about this," Darrell said as he handed me a folded-up magazine.

"What is this?" I said, taking it. I opened it to see it was the *National Enquirer*.

"Check out page twenty-three," J. Love snapped.

He stood there as I read it. Sheridan and Kennedi looked over my shoulder.

"He's a hot R & B singer who's made a name for himself with his tributes to women, but it seems Miami singer J. Love is as fake as a three dollar bill. According to Maya Morgan, the host of the popular gossip show, *Rumor Central,* J. Love is trying desperately to cover up a sexual assault charge he's facing in Seattle, Washington." I stopped reading. "What? No! I didn't do this!"

"So, they're lying on you?" J. Love asked. "Funny, they got you quoted." He jabbed at the paper. "They know all about me getting arrested and everything."

"I didn't do this." The magazine was literally shaking in my hands. "I swear, J. I didn't do this."

"Whatever. Usually, I don't play around with tricks who try to play me. You're lucky I'm not the old J. Love"—he leaned in and whispered in my ear—"or that pretty face wouldn't be so pretty anymore." He straightened up, brushed his jacket down. "But I got an image to uphold, so I'm gonna let you slide. This time. But if you know what's good for you, you will make sure you don't come anywhere near me."

"Are you serious, J?" I wanted to cry. I couldn't believe this.

"Do I look serious, Maya?"

"But I didn't do anything."

He gave me a look that showed he obviously didn't believe me as he walked off.

"Maya, what's going on?" Sheridan asked.

"Yeah, what is that?" Kennedi pointed to the balled-up magazine in my hand.

"I don't know. It's an article in the *National Enquirer,* and it quotes me, saying J is trying to cover up a sexual assault charge. And that he got arrested."

"I didn't know he got arrested," Sheridan said.

I looked uneasily at Kennedi. Sheridan would have a stroke if she knew I had told Kennedi about this and not her, and right now, I couldn't deal with that. Kennedi told me with her eyes though that she hadn't said a word to anyone.

"Nobody knew but him and me. And whoever he told," I said. "His attorney kept it out of the news." I ran my hands through my hair. I needed to figure out what in the world was going on.

"Well, it's obviously in the news now," Sheridan said.

"Yeah, thanks to you," this girl standing off to the side said.

"Would you get out of our conversation?" Kennedi snapped at her.

The girl rolled her eyes. "I don't blame him. I wouldn't invite you in either."

Suddenly, someone called out, "Maya!" All three of us turned toward the front door of the club to see the two girls Kennedi and Sheridan had gotten into it with earlier. "Yeah, we're about to go in! Why don't you guys give us your phone number so we can text you and let you know how the party is." They cracked up laughing as the bouncer let them inside.

Chapter 16

I had tossed and turned all night long. Kennedi, who had been sleeping next to me, finally sat up.

"What is wrong with you?" she said. She glanced over at the clock. "It's four in the morning!"

I threw back the covers and got up and began pacing. "It's this party. I can't get over what happened."

"Really? Yes, it was embarrassing as all get-out. But it's over. Go to bed." Kennedi turned on her side and pulled the covers over her.

"No," I said, flipping on the light next to my bed. "It's not just the not being able to get into the party. I don't want J. Love thinking I told his business."

"That's what you do," Kennedi said from beneath the covers. "You tell people's business. Why are you trippin' about it now?"

"But that's just it, I didn't tell the *Enquirer* anything. That doesn't make sense. If anything, I would have run the story myself, but I was really feeling J. Love. I would've never done anything like this! Are you sure you didn't say anything to anyone?"

She turned over and looked at me. "Again, I swear on my mama, my daddy, and everything I love, I didn't tell a soul. You know me. I wouldn't do that to you."

I sighed heavily. I knew she wouldn't. Kennedi was ride-or-die. "I know. I just need to figure out how I got caught up in this mess." I know Kennedi was tired of hearing that. I'd said it all the way home and until she fell asleep on me last night. But this had me devastated.

Kennedi let out a long sigh, then sat up. It was obvious I wasn't going to let her sleep, so I guess she decided to humor me.

"Well, the *Enquirer* said they got it from you," she said.

"Well, they didn't."

"Then I guess you need to find out why they're saying that."

"That's exactly what I'm going to do."

She patted my hand. "Maya, I believe you didn't do it, but you definitely need to find out who did." She yawned, then stretched. "But guess what? You can't do it at four in the morning, so why don't you go to bed? Figure it out tomorrow." She fell back, pulling the covers back over her head.

It was barely 8 a.m., but I was on my way to the station. I knew Tamara would be there because she had a 9 a.m. meeting that she'd been complaining about all week. I'd left Kennedi asleep. I'd tried to wake her up and ask her if she wanted to come with me, and she'd all but cursed me out.

I swung into the station's parking lot. I needed to catch Tamara before she headed to her meeting. I got her just as she was gathering up her stuff on her desk.

"Hey, Tamara, can I talk to you real quick?"

"What are you doing here on a Saturday?"

"I need to talk to you."

"Well, can't it wait? I'm running late for my meeting. Can't believe they are actually meeting on a freaking Saturday," she mumbled as she picked up her organizer and moved from behind her desk.

"Please, Tamara. This is important."

The look on my face must've told her how serious this was for me, because she stopped and said, "Hey, what's going on? Are you in some kind of trouble?" She put her stuff down and sat in the chair in front of her desk.

I sat down in the chair next to her and quickly recapped what had happened at the party last night.

"So all of this is because you didn't get into J. Love's party?"

"No, it's not that at all. It's because the *Enquirer* said I gave them this story, and I didn't have anything to do with it."

"Well, why does J. Love think you do?"

I pulled out the magazine and handed it to Tamara. It was already opened to page twenty-three. Tamara read the story, then looked up at me. "If you had this kind of information, why would you give it to them? Why wouldn't you air it on *Rumor Central?*"

"Exactly," I said. "That's what I was trying to tell him. If I were going to release this information, it wouldn't be through the *National Enquirer.* I wouldn't give this type of story to someone else."

"So why does he think you're behind it?"

I jabbed the paper. "You see my name? They're directly quoting me."

"And you didn't talk to anyone from the *Enquirer?*"

"No," I protested. I took a deep breath, trying to calm myself down. "I was hoping you could call and see where they really got this information from."

She nodded. "Well, I do have a contact over there. Hold on." She picked up the phone and punched some numbers in. After a brief hesitation, she said, "Hey, Michelle. It's Tamara Collins over at WSVV. How are you? . . . Yeah, me too. Well look, I won't hold you long. Just trying to get some info on a story you guys ran on that singer, J. Love. It's actually being attributed to one of my employees." Tamara paused, looked in my direction. "Yeah, her."

"Put her on speakerphone," I whispered. I needed to know what was going on before I went crazy.

Tamara looked unsure for a minute, then put the handset down and pressed the button to put it on speakerphone.

Michelle was midsentence. ". . . So, we actually all kinda wondered why she was giving the story to us instead of airing it there. But we figured it was personal, since rumor had it she was dating him. Why, what's up?"

"Maya was directly quoted, but she denies ever talking with anyone there."

"Of course she'd say that." Michelle laughed. "She doesn't want you mad that she gave the story to us."

I jumped up. "I didn't—"

Tamara quickly shushed me, and I sat back down, fuming.

"No, Michelle. I know Maya. She is adamant that she never talked with anyone over there. That she never told anyone this story, period," Tamara said.

I heard a bunch of shuffling, like Michelle was looking through some papers. "Hold on. I'm looking at the notes here. . . . Yep. It says all communication was done via email."

"I didn't email anyone," I whispered.

"Shhh," Tamara said, putting her finger to her lips.

"Well, what email address is it showing that the information came from?"

"Hey, this is all off the record, right?" Michelle asked.

"Yeah, girl. You know I'm not going to get you in any trouble."

"GossipGirl2013." Michelle said. "That's where everything came from."

I fell back in my seat, stunned. That was my email address.

"Hey, look, Tamara, I hope she's not trying to get a retraction or anything, because everything on our end looks legit."

"Nah, we were just wondering," Tamara said.

"Do you want me to have the reporter who did the story call her?"

I nodded.

"Yeah, can you have him call her? Because this is a little scary to her," Tamara said, then rambled off my cell phone number.

"All right, will do."

Tamara ended the call and looked at me.

"That's my email address, but I didn't send it," I mumbled.

"So if you didn't send it, who did?"

"That's what I would like to know."

"Does anyone have access to your email?"

I thought about Jayla, but I hadn't given her my email address, let alone the password to that. She only had my social media information. Besides, why would she try to set me up? Maybe Bryce was behind all of this. It didn't seem like something he would do, but since he'd found out about J. Love and me, maybe he was trying to get revenge. Even still, how would he have known about the arrest?

"I don't know who did it." I stood. I was getting angry all over again. "But I tell you what, I'm not resting until I get to the bottom of this."

Tamara stood, too, and gathered her stuff up again. "Okay. Let me know what you find out. I need to get to the studio."

I followed Tamara out, almost in a daze. No way would J. Love ever trust me again, even if I proved it hadn't been me, which I had no idea how I could do. That relationship was as good as over, I told myself. But this was bigger than J. Love. Someone was playing with my life now, and I wouldn't rest until I found out who it was.

Chapter 17

"Maya, someone's asking about you," one of my classmates said as I walked through the double doors that led outside. I'd tried to relax over the weekend, but this whole *National Enquirer* thing had consumed me. Kennedi got so mad at me that she ended up going back to Orlando early. I couldn't help it, I needed to figure this thing out. I'd tried to call J. Love, but of course, he wouldn't answer my calls. Bryce had answered and had gone off on me when I asked him if he had hacked into my email. I even asked Jayla about it, and she confirmed that she only had passwords to my social media stuff.

"Who is it?" I asked my classmate.

She shrugged. "I don't know. Some funny-looking old dude."

I made my way over to where she was pointing. The strange man was leaning against my car. He was frumpy looking in a too-small tweed blazer and some tight brown khakis.

"Maya Morgan?" he asked as I got a little closer.

"Yes?"

He held his hand out for me to shake. "Pleasure to meet

you." His eyes roamed up and down my body for a quick second. "Such a shame I had to work and toil for years to get a foot in the door, and look at you, all big-time and you're not even old enough to buy a beer."

I narrowed my eyes at him. Was that some kind of back-handed compliment?

"But I guess that's what a lot of money and a pretty face can get you, though," he cackled.

"What can I do for you?" I didn't have time for this mess.

"My boss said you wanted to talk to me." He pulled out a business card. "Edward Sternham, reporter for the *National Enquirer.*"

Oh, this was the reporter I wanted to talk to. Great! I took the card. "Thank you so much for coming to talk to me, Mr. Sternham. But we could've done that over the phone. I hate that you had to come to my school."

"Well, I was passing by your school, and I thought, let me take my chances. I was gonna come to the TV station, but I knew you were probably at school. Besides, don't know if I want to go to that station. They never would hire me, you know?"

It took everything in my power not to roll my eyes. "Well, Mr. Sternham, I had some concern about the story you ran about the singer, J. Love."

He grabbed his belt loops and pulled up his pants like they were actually falling. "Yeah, well, I'd like to thank you for that tip."

"The only thing is, I didn't give you that tip."

He looked at me in surprise. Then pulled out a notepad. "Is your email gossipgirl2013@gmail.com?"

I nodded.

"Well, that's where the tip came from. And when I emailed for permission to use your name, you gave me the go-ahead. I got a paper trail. It's all in writing."

I sighed. "So, you just take a story via email and run with it without ever actually talking to anyone?"

He seemed offended. "Look here, little lady. Don't tell me how to do my job. I have been doing this for twenty-one years. I know what I'm doing. You gave me the tip and the quote, but I verified that the story was legit all on my own."

"I'm sorry, Mr. Sternham." I wasn't trying to upset him. Not before I got some answers. "This is all just very upsetting to me, because it wasn't me who sent the email. Do you have any more information?"

He stood for a minute, like he was in a face-off. But then, he relaxed, "Nope, your email just gave me the tip and the quote, and I took it and dug up the rest of the information. That's what I do." He paused and stared at me again. "Obviously, I don't do it as well as you, though." He tried to laugh.

"Well, that's why I said you could've saved yourself a trip. You could've just answered my questions over the phone. I was just trying to find out details on how you got the story, but it doesn't look like there's much you can tell me."

"Wish I could tell you more." He shrugged, looking like he really wished he could help me. But I could tell he was being fake.

"But, since I have you here, there is something I'd like to talk to you about. There's another story I'm working on."

I raised an eyebrow as he continued.

"Is your father Myles Morgan?"

"Yes," I said hesitantly. "Why?"

"Well"—he stroked his graying, bushy mustache—"I heard that he's being investigated for money laundering."

"What?" He was definitely talking about the wrong man.

"Yeah, word is Mr. Morgan is using his hotel chain to clean up some money for some high-powered folks, some folks involved in the drug game. So, I'm digging around, and

I thought, why not just go to the horse's mouth. Or the pony's." He had the nerve to pull his digital tape recorder out and point it at me. "So, do you know anything about your dad's money laundering?"

"You got my dad and me real twisted," I said with serious attitude. "He doesn't need to launder anything. And he dang sure isn't working with any drug people."

"Okay, don't get all testy." He paused. "Have you ever seen him involved in any illegal activity at all?"

"I think our conversation is done, and I'm going to need you to please leave me alone." I pushed him aside and tried to open my car door.

"Don't be like that," he said, jumping in front of me. "I mean, we're one and the same."

"I'm nothing like you," I said.

"Really, you are."

I got into my car. "Here's my card," he said. He dropped it in my lap before I closed my door. "Why don't you pass it to your dad and tell him I'd like an exclusive interview with him, since I'm sure you won't want to do the story yourself. I can do a one-on-one. You deal with those teenyboppers. This is grown folks business I'm talking about."

"Good-bye, Mr. Sternham."

He laughed as I shut my door on him and began backing away.

Money laundering? The only reason I knew what that was, was because I had watched this episode of *CSI* in which this man was taking drug money and funneling it through his company, trying to make it legitimate. But no way would my dad be caught up in some mess like that. My dad had always been on the up-and-up.

I couldn't help but wonder where Mr. Sternham was getting his information. Maybe the person who had lied on me was now lying on my dad. I spun out of the school parking lot. This was getting out of hand. Someone was trying to play with me, and Maya Morgan didn't get down like that. They'd picked the wrong one, because I wasn't going down without a fight. But first, I needed to clear up this mess with my dad.

Chapter 18

The silence in our house was driving me crazy, but still, I couldn't pull myself up from the kitchen table. I might not be able to find out who was behind the lies about me—yet—but I could get some answers from my father, if he ever got home.

After what seemed like another hour of waiting, I heard the lock turn in the door, and my parents finally walked in. My mom and dad were laughing and all hugged up. They were dressed up in after five attire, probably coming from one of their many charity events.

"Maya, it's eleven o'clock at night. What are you doing still up?" my dad asked when he noticed me.

"I've been waiting on you."

"For what?"

"I need to talk to you."

"About what, sweetie?" my mom said.

Suddenly, I wished I had waited until my mom had gone to sleep. I didn't need her fussing at me about bringing some mess like this to my dad. But it was too late.

"What's going on? Is everything all right?" my dad asked.

He walked over and stroked my hair. "You're not having any problems with that show, are you?"

"No, it's not that." I sighed heavily, then looked at my mom, then back at him. "Some reporter showed up after school today, trying to talk to me."

My mother frowned. "A reporter? From where?"

I paused, then stared directly at my father so I could see his reaction. "The tabloid magazine, the *National Enquirer.* He wanted to know if I knew anything about you laundering money. I mean, I can't believe that someone would think . . ."

The looks on my parents' faces stopped me cold. My mother began taking short, deep breaths like she was about to hyperventilate.

"Mom?"

She covered her mouth and ran from the room.

I jumped up from my seat. "Dad, what is going on? This reporter isn't telling the truth, is he? You're not caught up in any shady stuff, are you?"

My dad began pacing back and forth.

"Dad, tell me what's going on?"

I was getting scared now. The last thing I needed was my family's being caught up in some kind of criminal activity.

He blew a deep breath and pointed to my chair. "Have a seat, Maya."

I didn't move. "Dad, tell me that you're not doing anything wrong."

He grabbed my hands and squeezed them reassuringly. "Honey, I'm not. But, apparently, someone at the executive offices was. And they're trying to tie it to me."

"*They*? Who are *they?*"

"The FBI."

"Oh my God," I said, falling back in my seat. My friend Erica's dad had been arrested in some kind of pyramid scheme. Her family lost everything. Both of her parents were arrested, and she had to go live with relatives in Indiana. "Are you going to jail?" I asked, horrified. "You can't go to jail. My life would be ruined if you go to jail."

My dad actually laughed. "*Your* life would be ruined?"

"Do you know how embarrassing that would be?"

He smiled as he brushed my hair again. "Maya, I'm not going to embarrass you. We're fighting this."

"Why didn't you tell me this?" I cried. Never in a million years had I thought that reporter was telling the truth.

"Well, we didn't think this concerned you."

"If my dad is about to go to jail, it concerns me."

"Your dad isn't going to jail, because your dad didn't do anything wrong." He lifted my chin. "Sweetheart, I have a top-notch team of attorneys, and they are going to prove that I did nothing wrong."

I plopped my head down on the table. "Oh my God. My dad is a thug," I wailed.

He chuckled again. I didn't see how he found humor in any of this. "Your dad is not a thug. Your dad is still the same Harvard Business School graduate and CEO of Morgan Enterprises. I'm not about to jeopardize my company or my family by getting involved in any illegal activities."

Serious tears were streaming down my cheeks now. "They sent Martha Stewart to jail. T.I. and Snoop went to jail, too. They all are rich and had top-notch attorneys."

"I'm not any of those people. I didn't do anything wrong, except trust someone I shouldn't have trusted. But I promise, sweetie, everything is going to be okay."

"Okay, fine." I sniffed and wiped my tears.

He rubbed my head. "Don't you worry your pretty little head about this. It will all be taken care of."

It had better. The People's Choice Awards was coming up, and the last thing I needed was to have my name associated with any criminal activities. It was bad enough that my name was being sullied with this J. Love story. Having this hit the news would just send me over the edge.

Chapter 19

I groaned as I walked into the classroom. This is exactly why I didn't want to come to this stupid winter party planning meeting. But our school had some kind of bogus rule that every student had to put in two hours of service, and I'd been putting mine off, and if I wanted my service points, I didn't have any other choice.

But watching the way Shay and Evian were snarling at me, I thought I would've been better off just taking my F.

"Hey, Evian. Hey, Shay," Sheridan said.

"Hey, Sheridan," both of them said, not bothering to look my way.

Oh, screw that. I was already on the edge, and I wasn't going to let their catty ways get to me. I'd been stressed over my dad all night. Tamara had told me the *National Enquirer* wouldn't print a retraction like I had hoped on the J. Love story. So, if I had to deal with any attitudes today, I just might snap. That's why I forced a smile and said, "Hello, girls."

They both slowly turned their heads my way, then looked back at Sheridan.

"Why is she speaking to us?" Shay asked.

When I was a little girl, my grandmother used to always say you get more flies with sugar, so I kept being nice.

"I'm speaking because that's the thing you do when you walk into a room with people. You say hello."

"Is she still talking to us?" Shay said.

I finally lost my smile. "Look—"

"Come on, guys," Sheridan said, jumping in. "It's time we squash this."

Shay raised an eyebrow at her. Evian rolled her eyes. I massaged my temple.

"Come on, guys," she protested. "We all were good friends."

"No, *you* were good friends with her," Shay said, folding her arms across her chest.

"Well, we all were at least cool," Sheridan corrected. "We run in the same clique."

"Oh, not anymore," Shay said. "Your girl is too large to hang with us anymore."

"Yeah," Evian echoed. "She's too good to hang with us, I guess."

I started to just get up and walk out, but I was tired of the 'tude, so I said, "Look, I don't know what you guys expected or wanted me to do. I'm sorry if it seems like I stabbed you all in the back. I wasn't trying to do that."

Both of them seemed a little shocked. Probably because they knew Maya Morgan didn't normally apologize.

I turned to Evian. "Evian, you're here. You're not behind bars; you're not being investigated. If I had wanted to get you in trouble, I could've easily given your name in the story. I didn't put you anywhere in it."

"Yeah, but you messed with my business."

"Come on, you had told me yourself that you were tired of doing that." Evian's uncle had actually been the brains behind the little escort ring, but Evian had been in charge of getting and managing the girls from high school. I'd run the story on my show, but I hadn't mentioned names.

Evian paused, then said, "That's beside the point. Plus, you don't know the drama you created with my uncle." She looked at me pointedly. "And you don't know how I saved your behind."

That made my heart skip. Rumor had it that Evian's family was attached to the Mafia. She would never confirm that, but I didn't want to mess around, so I said, "Thank you for that."

"I don't care about her apologies," Shay said. "You sold us out for your own little fame, after you were the one talking that mess about us being a team and sticking together, when we were going through negotiations that I didn't even want to do."

Out of everyone, Shay was the angriest with me. We had been up for contract renewals for our reality show, *Miami Divas.* I had convinced everyone to fight for more money and perks. Shay hadn't wanted to do that, because it's not like any of us needed the money. But I had tried to tell them it was the principle of it all. But instead of meeting our demands, the network had canceled the show and offered me my own. I don't know what I was supposed to do, but I did the only thing that made sense; I took the offer and said "deuces" to my team. So, quiet as it's kept, I understood Shay's anger. But she needed to get over it, because it is what it is.

"I didn't sell you guys out. When they came to offer me a show, they said they just wanted me. What was I supposed to say, 'Oh, no, I'm not going to take it because of my friends'?" I said.

Evian and Shay glared at me. "No, it's the foul way you did it," Shay said. "That's what I have a problem with."

"And Bali was our boy, and your actions caused him to be shipped away," Evian added.

Out of everything that went down, that bothered me the most. I really liked Bali and hated that his father had found out he was even remotely connected to the Bling Ring, a group of teens who were breaking into and vandalizing celebrity homes. He'd shipped Bali back to Cuba so fast it was crazy. I'd hoped Bali would return, but so far, no one had heard from him.

"I wasn't trying to get anyone in trouble," I said.

"I'd hate to see what you did if you tried." Shay turned up her lips. Evian seemed to soften, but Shay looked like she wasn't trying to hear anything I had to say.

A silence hung in the air for a minute, then Sheridan said, "So are we good?"

Evian and I nodded. Shay flicked us off and picked up the agenda that was sitting in the middle of the oval table.

"What are we supposed to be doing?" Shay said. "I don't want to do this whack winter dance planning anyway."

"Yeah, we're supposed to just show up and look fabulous," Evian said.

"I heard Nicole say we're waiting on one more person," Sheridan said as we took seats at the table with Evian and Shay.

We all sat around for a minute waiting for the committee chair, Nicole, to come in. Finally, a smile crossed Shay's face. "So, you and Bryce aren't together anymore?" she asked me.

"Noooo," I said slowly, wondering where she was going with that. "And?"

"So, you don't care about him kickin' it with someone else." She shrugged nonchalantly, but I could tell she was taking great pride in this.

"Kickin' it with who? Callie? I couldn't care less about that little homely thing."

"Oh, I'm not talking about Callie." Shay smirked.

"Well, who then?" I looked at Sheridan.

"Don't look at me," she said. "I'm not thinking about Bryce."

"Oh, it ain't Sheridan either." Shay laughed. "But it is someone else you know. Your number one fan."

"Who?"

Evian and Shay looked at each other and giggled. "Who else wants to be like you so bad that she transferred to your school, dyed her hair jet-black to match yours, and now she's trying to take your man."

"Jayla?" It was my turn to laugh. "First of all, she didn't transfer because of me, and, secondly, Bryce wouldn't mess with someone like her. And even if he did, it wouldn't matter, because he isn't my man. I've moved on to bigger and better things."

"Oh, yeah, like J. Love," Evian said with a slick smile.

"Oh, wait, is he still with you?" Shay was trying to play dumb, but I could tell she knew the whole story. Those stupid girls who were filming us posted it on Facebook; it went viral, and everyone at school had seen us getting turned away from the party. "Because after you sold him out to the tabloids, and couldn't get into his party, I heard he dumped you."

"You guys, stop," Sheridan said.

"Why? She can dish it, but she can't take it?" Shay stood and started gathering her stuff. "Whatever. You guys can sit here and kiss and make up and sing "Kumbaya," but Maya is foul." She looked me up and down. "And I for one ain't gon' forget it." She turned to Evian. "Tell Nicole I'll make up my points at the next meeting."

I let her go. Shay was the least of my concerns. Was there any truth to what she had been saying? And if there was, could I even get mad? By the time Jayla had transferred here, I had already broken up with Bryce. And yeah, she had seen the little exchange in English class several days ago, but if she hadn't known about Bryce and me, she might not have even been aware that we used to be an item. Even still, it burned my heart to think of her being with him. I wasn't about to let Bryce know I cared, but I was definitely about to get some answers from Jayla.

Chapter 20

I looked up just as Jayla came bouncing over to my lunch table, where Sheridan and I were finishing up our lunches. I hadn't really paid attention to her before, but Evian was right. Her hair, which used to be dark brown, was now the same dark shade as mine. Her layered cut was real close to mine, and that baby-doll T-shirt, the boyfriend jacket, and those skinny jeans looked like something straight out of my closet. Could she really be trying to imitate me?

"Hey, Maya," Jayla said. Her usual giddy smile had returned. "Sorry about the other day. I was PMSing, so I wasn't in a good mood. I shouldn't have taken that out on you." The difference in her attitude was like night and day.

My first instinct was to go off about Bryce, but something stopped me. I needed to remember the source of this information.

"It's cool," I said dryly.

"Are you sure? Because you seem like something's wrong," she said, losing her smile and just standing in front of my lunch table like Debbie Dumbo.

I just side-eyed her until she sat down. She looked back and forth between Sheridan and me. "Is something wrong?"

She stared at me for a minute. "Are you mad at me for the way I acted?"

I dropped my fork and leaned back. "Do I have a reason to be mad?"

"I apologized for acting funky."

"I'm not trippin' over that."

"Then, what's wrong? If this is about the tweet I sent out this morning, I sent it to you for approval."

I usually tweeted my own stuff, but every now and then, she'd tweet for me. But she made sure to get my approval on everything before she sent it out.

"This isn't about some tweet," Sheridan snapped. "This is about her man."

"J. Love?"

"You know doggone well who her boyfriend was," Sheridan snapped.

Jayla looked at Sheridan, then back at me. "Maya, I have no idea what she's talking about," Jayla finally said.

I picked my fork back up and began toying with my salad. "A little birdie told me that you were pushing up on Bryce."

"Bryce, the football player, Bryce?"

"You know exactly who she's talking about," Sheridan snapped.

"Yeah, I saw that little exchange in English class the other day, but I didn't know what that was about. And he's in my sixth-period class. He's my lab partner."

"Oh, how convenient," Sheridan said.

Jayla still had a confused look on her face.

"Maya, what is going on? You're dating Bryce?"

"*Dated*, as in past tense," I said.

"Don't act like you don't know." Sheridan rolled her eyes. "You know everything there is to know about Maya. You probably know her bra size."

Jayla turned toward me, ignoring Sheridan. "I didn't

know, but honestly, I'm not trying to talk to Bryce," she protested. Her eyes were wide, like she was appalled at the idea. "Who told you that?"

"Don't worry about who told us."

"Sheridan," I said, "let me handle this. Weren't you about to go to class?"

Sheridan groaned. "Really, Maya? You're not gonna believe her, are you?"

I glanced across the cafeteria and caught Shay smiling as she watched me.

"Let me deal with this," I repeated to Sheridan.

Sheridan stood, snatched her tray up, and shook her head like I was pitiful.

As soon as she walked away, Jayla turned back to me. "Maya, I am so serious. I'm not trying to talk to Bryce, and I *didn't* know that you guys were together."

"Was he flirting with you?"

"He wasn't even flirting with me. Mr. Pittman put him as my lab partner. Bryce was just being nice."

I looked back over at Shay, who was now giggling with Evian.

Jayla's eyes began watering up. "Maya, you've got to believe me. I would never do you like that."

I sighed. I couldn't believe that I'd let that trick, Shay, trick me. "Nah, it's cool. It's not like Bryce and I are even together. My bad." I smiled. "So, what's been going on?"

She was quiet for a minute, but then her shoulders sank in relief, and she seemed to relax a little.

"Wait until you see this website I've designed." She pulled her laptop out of her bag and opened it. "I don't know if you've seen Tyra Banks's website," she said as she started punching keys on her MacBook. "But I wanted to model your site after that. It's an interactive 3-D site."

She turned the laptop around so I could see it better. My

mouth dropped open in awe as a 3-D image of me strutted across the screen, then stopped in the corner and said, "What's up, everyone? It's the ultimate gossip girl! The diva dishing the dirt. Make sure you check us out every week on *Rumor Central!*"

Jayla studied me as I watched it. It was as if she was really hoping I liked it. "Oh my God," I said. "Jayla, it's awesome!"

She smiled proudly. "I'm glad you like it. I've been working on it for a while. I was hoping you'd like it."

"Like it? I love it. You are so talented." I sifted through the website some more. This had to be one of the best websites I had ever seen. I mean, it still had my regular column, Get the Scoop, so I could still post the latest celebrity gossip and photos, but the 3D me took things to a whole other level. "How did you get into this?" I asked.

She shrugged. "I'm just a tech person."

"Did you take classes?"

"Nah, I taught myself." She closed her laptop and dropped it back in her bag. "I like computers. My dad wants me to major in computer engineering, but engineering is so boring."

"Well, whatever you choose, you definitely will do well. When does this site go live?"

"We're hoping by the end of the week, because Tamara said you're picking up seven more markets next week, so we want the site live by then."

I stood and gathered up my tray. "Well, this is amazing."

"Hey, I'm just grateful to be working with you." She smiled admiringly. "I love you, and this is just a dream come true."

I don't know why, but her words sent an eerie feeling through me. *Love?* She didn't know me like that. But I quickly shook it off. I was sure she was just speaking generally. I have fans tell me all the time that they love me, but I doubt any of them mean that literally.

"Well, we are lucky to have you." We laughed, and I couldn't help but notice the shocked look on Shay's face. She probably wanted some drama to jump off so she could be the first one taping it and uploading it to WorldStarHipHop.com. I was so glad I followed my gut. It would be a cold day before I let Shay Turner get the best of me.

Chapter 21

Today was one of those days when I wished that I could just crawl back in bed. We had had a long taping last night, and I was exhausted. I thought again about just dropping out of school, but I quickly nixed that thought, since dumb wasn't cute. Besides, it's not like my dad would cosign that anyway.

I dragged myself to my second-period class. I knew my first-period teacher was going to have a stroke, but I was moving as fast as I could. I had just turned the corner to head to my classroom when I looked up to see Shay Turner charging my way.

She body-slammed me into the lockers. The move quickly snapped me out of my daze, and I snatched a handful of her hair and tried to pull her off of me.

Tears were streaming down her face as she clawed at me. Someone, I have no idea who, pulled her off of me, but she kept swinging like a wild woman. "You . . . you . . ." She couldn't even catch her breath.

"What is wrong with you?" I screamed.

I could barely get up off the ground before she lunged at me again. Someone grabbed her again and pulled her off me.

The vice principal, Mrs. Young, came racing toward us. "What is wrong with you?" she yelled at me.

"Me? She's the one who charged me!" I shouted.

"You low-down . . ." Shay cried as she lunged toward me again. "Is this how you try to get me back?"

I jumped back out of her reach. I didn't back down from a fight, but I also wasn't a fool. I didn't fight crazy people, and right now, Shay was certifiably crazy. "What did I do now?"

Before either of us could say anything else, we were both shuttled into the principal's office. I couldn't believe this. I guess the principal couldn't either.

"Do you two want to explain to me what is going on?" Mr. Carvin asked once we were both seated in front of his desk. "Are you trying to get kicked out of school and not be able to graduate?"

"I was walking down the hallway minding my business when this fool came out of nowhere and attacked me!" I yelled. It was then that I tasted blood. Had this heffa busted my lip? I had to host an event tonight! I couldn't go in there with my lip all busted up!

Shay jumped out of the chair to try and go at me again. Luckily, the security guard stopped her.

"Miss Turner, what is your problem?" Mr. Carvin asked.

The guard pushed her back down in the chair, and Shay started sobbing. This was a side of her I hadn't ever seen. I'd seen her angry, but never crying. It was almost like she was truly hurt.

"Miss Turner, do you want to tell me what is going on?" Mr. Carvin repeated.

"She did it again," Shay cried, pointing at me. "I hate her."

"Shay, what are you talking about? I didn't do anything," I said.

"Not according to your stupid website."

"What are you talking about?"

"The story on your website. Don't play dumb."

"I'm not playing anything. What story?"

"You dishing the dirt," she said sarcastically. "You know you try to give us that whole game about you not selling out your friends, but you haven't changed. I mean, I know we're not friends anymore, but I just never thought that you'd do something like this."

"Shay, what in the world are you talking about?"

Mr. Carvin turned to me as well. "Miss Morgan, what have you done now?"

I threw my hands up. "I swear, I have no idea what she's talking about."

"You are so full of it." Before I knew it, Shay was out of the chair and coming toward me again. This time the guard grabbed her in a bear hug and pulled her kicking and screaming out of the office.

"Miss Morgan, wait right here," Mr. Carvin said, following them out.

I didn't know what Shay was talking about, but while they were trying to calm her down, I was going to figure it out. So I quickly got up, walked around to Mr. Carvin's computer, and logged onto the *Rumor Central* website. I was dumbfounded as a photo of Shay's mother—black eye and all—popped up, along with a photo of her father.

Miami hoopster accused of beating wife, the headline read. I pressed the link to get the story, and the little interactive me—that I thought was so cool just a few days ago—popped up.

"What's up? It's the ultimate gossip girl, Maya Morgan," the animated figure said. "Yes, your girl has dug up some more dirt. It seems NBA great Jalen Turner likes to slap his woman around. Check out how he jacked up the woman he promised to love 'til death did him part.'" Pictures of Shay's mother popped up again. Her left eye was black, and her face was all bruised. "*Rumor Central* obtained these photos of Jalen Turner's wife, and we learned he was taken into custody on domestic abuse charges. Remember, you heard it here first, and tune in to *Rumor Central* to get the latest scoop on this serious dirt." I fell back in the chair just as Mr. Carvin walked back in.

"Miss Morgan, do you want to tell me what is going on?" He saw the stunned expression on my face and walked over to his desk. He leaned in and clicked on the article. I winced as the interactive me repeated the story.

"Miss Morgan," he said, shaking his head as he closed the website out. "As much as I hate that rag of a job you have, I understand that you're just doing your job. But really, is this necessary?"

"Mr. Carvin, I know you won't believe me, but I didn't do this."

His expression told me that he definitely didn't believe me.

He pointed to the computer. "Is that not your website we just saw?"

I nodded.

"Is that little animated figure not you?"

"Yes, but—"

"Well, as much as I don't condone fighting, you're lucky Miss Turner didn't cause more damage."

I knew he was right about that. Shay was out for blood. I just sighed in defeat. I knew this whole "I didn't do it" was starting to sound played.

Chapter 22

This was getting ridiculous. First J. Love, now Shay. I did enough dirt digging on my own. I didn't need anyone attributing something I didn't do to me. And Sheridan was right about one thing. I didn't start having these problems until Jayla came around. That's why I was speeding toward her house right now. I hoped this stupid Google Maps didn't send me all over the place.

I was going to get to the bottom of this now. I'd tried to find Jayla at school, but I couldn't catch up with her. Then, one of her friends had told me she'd gone home early. As I drove to her house, it dawned on me that it was a good twenty minutes away; it made no sense that she would drive this far to come to Miami High.

I dialed her number again, and once again, it went straight to voice mail. I thought about calling Tamara, but I didn't need her trying to give me the "let me handle it" speech. This had gone too far, and Jayla was going to give me some answers whether she wanted to or not.

After getting turned around a few times, I finally found Jayla's place. Her car was there, so she'd obviously made it home.

I knocked on her door. No one answered, so I pulled out my phone and dialed her number again. Still no answer. For a minute, I thought maybe no one was there, but then I saw the curtain move like someone was peeping out.

"Jayla, open the door," I yelled. "I see you're in there."

"I'm coming," she called out. It took a few more minutes, but she finally opened the door. She had on a Hello Kitty bathrobe.

"Maya, what's up?" She caught me eyeing her robe and pulled it tighter. "I was taking a shower because I have some-where to be in a few minutes."

The look on her face answered my question. She knew I was here about Shay. She was absolutely terrified. I pushed past her and into her living room. Even though she was standing in the door as if she was trying to block me. "So I guess I know why you're not answering my calls."

"Wh-what are you talking about?" she stammered, fol-lowing me in.

I spun around to face her. "Wh-wh-what do you think?" I said, mocking her.

"Maya, it's not like that at all," she said, all flustered.

"Not like what? You're the only person that can go in the website and change stuff."

She stopped, frowned, then said, "Wait a minute, what are you talking about?"

It was my turn to frown. "I'm talking about the *Rumor Central* website. What did you think I was talking about?"

I swear, I saw a look of relief pass over her face, and then she said, "No, I mean, I thought that's what you were talking about. I just didn't understand what you were mad about."

"You don't understand? I'm mad because of this blatant lie you posted about Shay Turner's dad, attributing it to me."

"What are you talking about?"

"The article on Shay Turner's dad." Her and this dumb

act. And if she tried to give me some bull about being hacked, I was gonna scream.

"Yeah, what about it?" Jayla said, looking at me confused.

So, she wasn't going to deny it? I had been prepared for her to start giving me excuses about being hacked.

"Oh, so you admit putting it up?"

"Yeah," she slowly said. "And the problem would be?"

My mouth dropped open. "Why would you put that up there?"

She looked at me in confusion, like I was speaking a foreign language. "Ummm, because you told me to."

"What? I didn't tell you to do anything."

"You sent me an email last night. All the details were in there, and you said post it ASAP. You told me not to change anything."

"I didn't send any email." Okay, this was getting ridiculous.

"Yes, you did. About seven last night."

"At seven last night, I was in the middle of an appearance for the TV station. What did the email say?"

She walked over to her laptop and punched a few keys, before turning the laptop around to face me. I set my phone down, leaned in, and read. Jayla, I need you to post this story in the Get the Scoop section. Run as is. I'm at an event so I can't call, but I need it to go up ASAP.

"I didn't send this!" I protested. I looked up at the email address. It was definitely my email address. "This is too much. Someone keeps hacking into my email account."

"I'm sorry. I just did what it said."

"Why wouldn't you call me to verify the story?"

"I don't ever call. You always just send me the stuff via email, and I post it."

I took a deep breath. I wanted to be mad, but she was right. That was how I usually did it. Now the question was, who in the world was hacking into my account?

"So you didn't send the email?" she asked.

"No, I did not."

"Wow," she said.

I ran my fingers through my hair. This was all getting to be too much. "I don't know what's going on. I've got to get to the bottom of this."

"Do you want me to change your password?" she asked.

"Yeah, like right away."

"Okay." She started easing toward the door. "Well, I'll get that changed right away. If there's anything else I can do to help, let me know."

"Yeah, fine. Sorry for trippin' with you."

"Okay, no problem." She held the door open. When she noticed me looking at her strangely, she said, "Sorry to rush you, but I really need to get going."

"Fine. I'll talk to you later."

I'd barely set foot outside before she was closing the door behind me. Forget her. I had bigger fish to fry. I needed to figure out how someone was hacking into my account.

I had just turned off Jayla's street when I realized that I had left my phone on her table when I set it down to look at her laptop.

"Doggone it," I said, making a U-turn so I could go back and get it. I parked in front of Jayla's house and made my way back up her walkway. I was just about to knock on her door when it opened.

To say I was shocked was an understatement. Standing there in the doorway was my ex, Bryce. He and Jayla were laughing, but when they noticed me, they stopped cold.

"Maya!" Jayla said, coming around in front of him. She now had on a T-shirt and some shorts. I couldn't do anything but stare. I looked back and forth between the two of them.

"Is this why you were rushing me out?"

"It's not like that at all. I know this looks bad, but it's nothing."

"Are you kidding me?" I said.

"No, I'm serious. It's not like that at all. Bryce was here helping me. I mean, we are lab partners, and he was helping me with my project."

"I guess that's why you were in your robe?"

"No. . . . But, I mean, I had to change out of my school clothes, and that's when you knocked, and that's when . . ." It sounded like every word coming out of her mouth was a lie.

"So were you hiding?" I asked him.

"No, he went upstairs to use the bathroom."

"Bryce can't speak for himself?"

He glared right back at me, then tried to shrug like he couldn't care less. "Yo, it's like she said; it's not even like that."

"What's it like, Bryce?"

He looked like he was about to explain, then I don't know if ego took over or what, because he said, "Nah, I wasn't hiding. What I got to be hiding for? What's it to you anyway? I'm here kickin' it with her. *And?* It's not like we're together anyway."

"Wow," I said.

Jayla turned and gave him the evil eye. "Are you serious, Bryce?"

He pulled her close to him and put his arm around her neck. "Nah, what we got to lie for? I'm single. You're single. What difference does it make to her?"

"Wow," I repeated. Bryce would get no more of my time. I stared directly at Jayla. "You're such a big fan that you got with my ex. Really? Slut."

"Why she gotta be a slut?" Bryce said. Was he seriously defending her?

"Maya, please. I'm sorry," Jayla cried, pulling away from him.

My first instinct had been to slap her. But Bryce wasn't my man, and any secret hopes I had of us ever getting back together were definitely gone. "Both of you can kiss my—"

"Maya, please?" she begged. "Don't be mad."

"Whatever, Jayla." I spun around and walked away. I'd just buy a new phone. I just needed to get away. I didn't care if I ever saw Bryce again. And the same went for that backstabbing trick, Jayla.

As hard as I tried to act though, the minute I turned off Jayla's street, I couldn't help but break down in tears.

Chapter 23

I would never in a trillion years admit this to anyone, but I cried myself to sleep last night. I think a part of me had held out hope that this was just another one of Bryce's and my many breakups to make up. Even with me kickin' it with J. Love—before everything went down anyway—my heart still belonged to Bryce, and I knew, eventually, we'd get back together. But there was no way I could get back with him now. Not after I knew he'd been with *her*. And he knew that she worked for me. That was about as lowdown as they came.

My phone rang, and I almost didn't answer it, but I knew it was Kennedi. I had talked on the phone with her last night until three in the morning. I knew she was worried and calling to make sure I was okay, so I went ahead and answered.

"Hello."

"Hey, *chica*. You all right?"

"I'm cool. I told you last night. I'm not even trippin' over him."

"Tell that to someone who doesn't know you," she replied. "But the question is, what are you gonna do about it?"

I fell back across my bed. "There's nothing for me to do.

Like he said, we're not together, so it's no biggie. I'm moving on."

"As well you should," she said. "But you also shouldn't let that freak come in and steal your man."

"Bryce is not my man."

Kennedi didn't pay my protests any attention as she kept talking. "I told you I didn't have a good feeling about her. She wants to be you so bad that she's settling for your sloppy seconds."

"Yeah, I'm gonna deal with her, but can we talk about something else?" As much as I wanted to beat Jayla down, that wasn't my style. But I fully intended to have her fired immediately.

"Fine," Kennedi huffed. "But you better tell her about herself or I will."

"Can we please talk about something else?" I repeated.

"Okay, well, I have some news that will make you smile."

"What?"

"I may be coming back to Miami."

That made me sit straight up. "What?"

"That's right," she squealed. "My dad is opening a branch for his bank there and said we may move back and be based out of there."

"Oh my God! That is so awesome." I stood and walked over to the picture of Kennedi and me at a party last year. We'd had the best time, and I'd gotten in so much trouble because I hadn't come home until six in the morning. "On second thought, I don't know if that's a good thing or a bad thing," I corrected.

"What is that supposed to mean?"

"You and me together on a regular basis? That's nothing but trouble."

"Trouble is my middle name."

We both laughed.

"Well, let me get out of here," Kennedi added. "I have to get to school. I just wanted to call and check on you."

"Thanks, Ken. But I'm cool."

"You need to be. Remember, you're in the big leagues now. A-list. Bryce is C-list. You don't need him. But I tell you what, I'm definitely going to need you to handle that chick."

"Yeah, you're right. That's the first mission this morning."

I hung up, then hurriedly got dressed. On my way to school, I whipped out my new phone and called Tamara.

"Hey, Maya," Tamara said, answering on the first ring. "What's going on?"

"It's Jayla," I said, cutting straight to the chase.

"What about her?"

"I want her gone. I don't want to work with her anymore."

"Maya, what are you talking about?"

"I just want her gone. Today." I didn't want to go into details, because I didn't want Tamara telling me how trivial I was being.

"Okay, I understand," she slowly said. "But it doesn't work like that. So what happened?"

I thought about what I should say, then just decided on telling her the truth. "I just caught Jayla with my ex."

"Caught her doing what?"

"Let's just say she was with him at her house, only wearing a robe, and he bragged about them being together. I'm not trippin' over him. He's a stank dog. But I can't work with someone I don't trust."

"Wow. I hate to hear that," Tamara said.

"It is what it is. But I'm not working with her."

"Whoa. I need you to slow your roll, Maya. And think about this."

I slammed my palm on the steering wheel. "There's nothing to think about. I want her gone!"

"Maya, I understand that you're emotional. But I've been in this business a while, and no one in the whole station, in the business, knows this social media and Internet stuff like Jayla."

"*And?*"

"And the reason you have a fan club with 200,000 members, the reason you have over a million likes on Facebook, the reason you have all of that, is because of Jayla."

"No, that's because of me."

She took a deep breath. "I'm not taking anything away from you, but my point is, half of those people wouldn't know about you if it weren't for Jayla. So we can't just up and let her go."

"Well, it's my show, and if I don't want to work with her, I shouldn't have to."

"Yeah, it's your show, but it's our investment. That's number one. Number two, the girl has a contract, which you insisted on by the way. So we can't just up and fire her without cause."

"We have a cause. Cause she's messing with my man." I quickly caught myself. "I mean, my ex-man, and she lied about it. And that makes me not trust her."

Tamara laughed. I didn't see anything funny. "My point is, we can't let personal beefs get in the way of business," she said. "I told you, you keep that personal stuff out there in the streets. What we do at this station is all about the Maya Morgan brand. And we're about bringing in the best people to build the Maya Morgan brand. And sorry, Jayla is the best."

"So, I'm just supposed to continue working with her?"

Tamara was quiet for a minute. Then, she said, "Okay, I'll tell you what. You can go through my assistant, Kelly. Anything you need from Jayla, or vice versa, will come through Kelly."

I wanted to protest some more, but I knew Tamara; nothing I said would get her to change her mind. "Whatever."

"Maya, I'm going to need you to understand, we are heading places. We just got syndicated. We can't be making changes now."

I didn't like it. But I understood. Jayla *was* the best. And Bryce was a buster. Why should my career suffer because of him?

"Fine. She can stay on. But if she says a word to me, it's on."

Tamara laughed. "You're not a violent person."

"Let that trick try me, and I might just become one," I couldn't help but add.

Chapter 24

"Ugggh," I said, tossing my phone back in my purse. I promised myself that was my last time trying to call J. Love. I couldn't come across as some stalker chick. Usually, I would've completely blown him off, but I just couldn't stand the fact that he thought I had sold him out. Not only was it messing with me personally, but I didn't need that getting around the entertainment industry; if it did, people wouldn't want to come on my show.

"Hey, Maya," Ava said, coming over to me as I got my book out of my locker for my sixth-period class.

"Hey." I really wasn't in the mood for Ava's bubbly personality.

"You are really going in, huh?"

I stopped and turned to her. "What? What are you talking about?"

"You tell me. I'm trying to figure out what's going on because of these crazy tweets."

"Again, what are you talking about?"

"My fans suck. So tired of this biz," she read, then held the phone up so I could see. The tweets were coming from MayaMorganGossipGirl. That wasn't my Twitter handle. But someone had created a fake Twitter account in my name. My problems just seemed to keep snowballing.

"Here comes your mini-me," Ava said as we saw Jayla walking down the hall.

"Maya, can I talk to you?" Jayla said, approaching me like nothing was wrong. She had on a brown BCBG warm-up that was just like my pink BCBG warm-up. I wouldn't be caught dead wearing it at school, but I had worn it when she came by my house one day. Had she run out and bought an outfit just like it? Oh my God, my friends were right. Jayla Cooper *was* trying to be me.

"If you know what's good for you, you would not be talking to me." I slammed my locker—hard—to emphasize my point.

"Maya, please . . . ?"

I turned to face her directly. Obviously, she was hard of hearing, so I got right up in her face. "Do. Not. Talk. To. Me."

She folded her arms defiantly. "No, I need to know what I did to you. I told you, you were reading too much into that Bryce situation. He only said we were messing around to make you mad."

I glared at her, then just began walking away since I was about six seconds away from punching her in the throat.

She jumped in front of me, blocking my path. "Seriously, tell me what I did to make you so mad."

This girl was some kind of special, and not in good way. "Are you like seriously asking me that question? Where do I start, you freak?"

She looked shocked.

Oh no, she wanted me to talk. I was about to talk. In front of a hallway full of people. I stepped back toward her. "You are a psycho stalker. And I'm not going to rest until you're gone."

This chick had the nerve to look appalled. "All I've ever tried to do was be your number one fan."

"With fans like you, who needs enemies?" I flicked her off and started to walk away again.

"You are so lowdown," she said to my back.

By now, we had an audience, and I wasn't about to let her punk me. "And you are such a freak. My friends were right. I should've never let your obsessive, creepy behind in my personal space. Get a life, and stay out of mine."

She looked like some kind of madwoman. "Ooooh, you are so gonna regret that."

"Whatever, loser. Go find someone else to harass. I hear Rihanna is in need of a fan club president." Several people laughed as I walked off. I hadn't intended to have such a vocal altercation. But just seeing her pushed my buttons. I had been jumped, dumped, denied entry into a party, and accused of stuff I hadn't done. . . . All of that in less than a month of knowing this chick.

"We'll see if you come off your high horse once you lose your precious little job," she spat.

I looked back over my shoulder. As if. *She* might be on the way out, but Maya Morgan was here to stay. There was no *Rumor Central* without me.

Chapter 25

It was taking everything in my power to just put my run-in with Jayla out of my mind and focus on my work. I'd been so caught up in all the drama that had become my life that I was way behind on digging up stories for the show. And my story for today had fallen through. I had exactly thirty minutes to find some juicy gossip for the Gossip Girl segment.

I sifted through the blogs, went through my contacts, trying my best to come across something that would spark an idea, but so far, nothing. I was just about to give up and tell my producer, Dexter, that I couldn't come up with anything, when Ariel walked in. She'd obviously come to her senses, because she'd apologized for her outburst and had been working extra hard.

"Hey, Maya, got a call when you were out." She looked at her notepad. "From Daysia McKinney's sister."

"Daysia McKinney, the reality TV star?"

"Yeah, it seems like they don't get along too well, and her sister was all too happy to let us know that Daysia has been arrested for shoplifting and got into a serious fight with the store clerk."

"Shoplifting? Daysia is rich."

"I know, but her sister says she has a serious cocaine habit, and her people had cracked down on her finances, so she took to shoplifting at a jewelry store, trying to support her habit."

"You talked to her?"

"I talked to the sister. I got the number for you. But she really doesn't want to talk because she's scared. She said she's emailing you the mug shot from Daysia's arrest so you can see her face all beat up from when she tried to fight the security guard. I'll give you the sister's number if you need to talk to her still."

"Let me see." I jumped back onto my computer and checked my email. "Yeah, it just came in," I said, seeing the email. I opened it and started reading. "Oh, this is good stuff," I said.

Ariel tried to lean over my shoulder and read the email. I looked up at her. "I got it from here."

She stepped back. "Sorry. Is there anything I can do?"

"I said, I got it. Thank you."

She glared at me like she wanted to say something more. But if she valued her job, she best to keep stepping.

"Excuse me, but I need to get on set in fifteen minutes," I said, when she still didn't move.

She nodded, and walked away, dejected. I let out a long sigh. Maybe I was too hard on her. Maybe I would look at her tape later. Maybe.

I turned my attention back to Daysia's story. This was major. Daysia was a breakout reality star who had crossed over to mainstream TV.

I called the research department and had them verify the arrest record. They were able to confirm it within five minutes, but they didn't have any other details. So, I couldn't go in-depth and run all this other stuff about the drug addiction, but I could use the picture and tease that viewers could find out more details later on the *Rumor Central* website.

I picked my phone up and dialed my producer, Dexter's, extension. "Hey, Dex. I found something to replace that story you pulled."

"Dang, girl. You're good. What is it?"

"It's a story on Daysia McKinney, the reality star. She was arrested for shoplifting and apparently has a drug habit."

"Wow, when did you find this out?"

"I just got it a minute ago."

"Did you get it vetted?" Even though it was gossip, our research department had to confirm that there was some element of truth to make sure we weren't running a bunch of lies.

"I haven't had time to confirm all the details because I need to get on set, but research did confirm the arrest, so I'm just going to run with that and the picture and tease the rest."

"Cool. I'll get an intro typed and let you take it from there and do your thing. See you on set in a few minutes."

I hung up the phone and reread the details of the email. If this stuff was true, Daysia was some kind of act. But I didn't have time to verify everything, so I would just go with the basics—for now.

I quickly touched up my makeup and headed to the set to do my thing.

Chapter 26

I saw Bryce and his teammate, Walter, walking toward me as I stood in the hallway in between classes. I immediately turned my head and pretended I was interested in what my friend, Chastity, was saying. I expected Bryce to keep walking past me, and I was actually shocked when he stopped right in front of me.

"You know, Maya, you always want to talk about somebody being foul and dirty. You're the queen of dirt."

I cut my eyes at him. "Bryce, why are you talking to me?"

"Because I'm sick of you and your harassing emails."

"Excuse me?"

"I ignored them the first few times, because I was gonna let you have your moment, since you're much more of a diva in your head than you actually are."

Part of me wanted to clean go off on him. But the other part was still stuck on "harassing emails."

"What are you talking about?" I asked.

"I'm talking about your emails."

"I haven't emailed you," I said, crossing my arms and giving him major attitude. "I don't have anything to say to your janky behind."

"Whatever, Maya. All I know is, email me again, and you'll see how much of a fool I can be."

He stomped past me. Oooh, he was making me so mad, but right now, I needed to put that aside.

"Bryce!" I called out after him.

"What, Maya?" He stopped, but didn't turn around.

I walked to catch up with him. "Would you turn around and listen?"

He slowly turned around.

"What are you talking about—what emails?"

Bryce huffed. "I don't know why you're trying to play all innocent."

"Think about it, Bryce. You claim to know me so well. Do I look like the type to harass anybody?"

He looked like he was thinking.

"Seriously, can I see these emails, Bryce?"

He got his phone out, tapped the screen, and then handed it to me.

You are such a nasty dog, I read. And you know how I do it. I don't get mad; I get even, and I got some dirt on your dad.

"What kind of dirt, Maya?" he asked, getting in my face. "What do you think you know? What kind of lies are you trying to spread on my pops?"

I held the phone out. "Are you for real, Bryce? Do you really think I wrote this?"

"It came from your email address."

"I don't care where it came from. I didn't write it. Someone has been hacking into my accounts and creating major havoc. You know I always text you. I don't send emails to you."

"Why would someone send this to me? I've been getting these for the last two weeks. And you seriously want me to believe that you didn't have anything to do with them?"

I was astonished. "The last two weeks? Why didn't you say anything?"

"I figured you were just being your usual bratty self, so I just deleted them. But now, you're pulling my dad into this, and I know what you did to Shay's dad. You know I don't get down like that."

"I didn't post the story about Shay. I didn't send you one single email. Matter of fact, the last time I said two words to you was that day you were over there hooking up with Jayla."

He turned up his lips, then let out a long sigh. "Jayla and I weren't doing anything. She offered to give me a ride to drop my car off at the shop. The only reason I said yeah was because we still needed to work on this science project. Then, she claimed she needed to go by her house to get something. Next thing I know, I look up, and she's talking about she needs to take a shower."

Bryce must think I'm Boo-boo the fool. "Really, Bryce? That's the best you can do?"

He shrugged. "I really don't care if you believe me or not. But that's what happened. Yeah, maybe I could tell what she was trying to do. And maybe I did think about getting with her, since I had just gotten an email from you talking about all the times you cheated on me. I was mad, so I maybe would've gotten with her, but then you showed up."

"Bryce, I didn't send any emails." I was beginning to wonder how well he even knew me. Because the one time I did cheat on him, that would go to my grave with me. I wasn't one of those confession type of chicks. "Jayla's doing all of this," I mumbled. "I know she is. She has to be behind everything."

"It's always someone else, isn't it, Maya?"

"Like you said, believe what you want to believe, Bryce. You were so quick to believe all the things Sheridan told you, and what happened? They were lies. This is a lie, too. But again, I don't care what you believe. I just wanted to know what was going on so I could get to the bottom of it."

I turned and spun off, stomping down the hall. For a minute, I thought he would come after me, but he didn't.

I couldn't even concentrate the rest of the day. Jayla had messed with the wrong one. I passed her in the hallway, and I debated snatching her up, but no, I needed to figure out a different way to get her back. I could understand her hacking into my account, now, after we'd fallen out. But the incident at her house was before all of that. And if she was such a fan, why was she trying to get with Bryce—unless it was all a game from jump. More and more, I was starting to feel like this was all some carefully orchestrated plan.

Chapter 27

Just when I thought my life couldn't get any worse, it did.

"Oh. My. God," Sheridan said, staring at the open magazine someone had conveniently left on my desk.

When I had first spotted it, I didn't know what it was. But now, there was no denying what this was. The magazine was open to the blaring headline: *Miami businessman's dirty money.*

Is this why people had been whispering and laughing as I walked to first period? I thought it was the usual hate, but now, I realized they had been laughing at me.

I snatched the magazine up, stuck it in my bag, and turned around and strutted out of the room. I wanted to race out in tears, but nobody was going to get that satisfaction.

"Young lady, where do you think you're going?" Mrs. Colson, my first-period teacher, said. I ignored her and kept walking. I didn't care what kind of trouble I got into, but I couldn't stay in this building one minute longer.

It was just my luck that I passed Shay and Evian on my way out. Both of them were snickering. I tried not to even look their way.

"Hey, Maya," Shay called out. "Saw the article on your dad. Bummer." She cracked up laughing.

I stopped and gritted my teeth as I fought back tears. I refused to cry.

"See, Evian, I told you. She can dish the dirt, but she can't take it," Shay said.

I glared at her. "Did you send this?" I asked, waving the magazine at her.

She rolled her eyes. "Please, you're the only one who gets off by talking about people's parents. I didn't have anything to do with this. But do I find it hilariously funny? Yep."

These people were really trying to break Maya Morgan. And for what? Because I was doing my job? I'd stopped doing stories on them, but they still hated on me. I had more secrets about each of them that I could tell, but I'd promised myself that I would keep my dirt digging out of my own backyard. Still, these people kept messing with me.

"Doesn't feel good when the dirt is about you, does it, Maya?" Shay added. "You want to tell everyone's business. Why didn't you tell people that your daddy is a crook?"

I couldn't help it. I stepped to her and said, "First of all, none of this garbage is true. Secondly, if it was, maybe your dad can give him some tips on how to stay out of jail, since that just so happens to be your dad's second home."

That wiped the smirk right off of her face. Still, she said, "Sweetie, the little weed charges my daddy gets in trouble for can't even compare to what your old man is about to go down for. That's some major penitentiary time." She shrugged. "But, hey, maybe you can do your show from Rikers Island or something, since that's where Daddy Dearest will be spending the rest of his life."

We stood face-to-face like those people in the old Westerns. I didn't know which of us would be the one to throw the first lick, but it was just a matter of seconds before one of us did.

Thankfully, Mr. Carvin's booming voice interrupted us.

"Ladies, I know you're not causing any trouble. Let's move it along. The bell has already rung."

Shay looked me up and down, then turned to Evian and laughed. "Come on, girl. No need to let her get under my skin. The way I see it, she has enough problems." They both cackled as they walked away.

I turned and headed toward the parking lot.

"Miss Morgan, your class is the other way!" Mr. Carvin called out. I ignored him, too. No way could I stay on this campus today. Thankfully, he didn't come after me.

I got in my car, pulled out of the parking lot, and didn't stop until I was parked in front of my house. I didn't even realize I'd been crying. This was so not cool. I needed to get it together. I was going down like some kinda sucka, and Maya Morgan didn't roll like that.

I noticed my dad's car, parked along with our attorney Herman's SUV and two other cars I didn't recognize. I parked and raced inside.

"Dad!"

All five men in our living room turned to me. My dad sighed heavily. He looked like he was in the middle of some intense conversation.

"Sweetheart, I'm sorry, but I really need to finish this meeting," he said.

"And I really need to know what's going on. You told me you would handle it. You told me there was nothing to worry about," I cried.

He walked over to me and took my hand. "There isn't."

I held up the *National Enquirer,* which was rolled up and clutched in my hand. "You're telling me this is nothing to worry about?" I said, shaking the magazine at him. "Someone put it on my desk at school."

Herman walked over to me as well. "Your dad is right, Maya. We are all over this."

"Dad, you said this wouldn't get out," I cried, ignoring Herman.

"No, I said we'd handle it, and we are," my dad said. "We can't concern ourselves with some erroneous tabloid reports."

"If it's not true, why are they printing it?"

My dad half-smiled. "You know all too well how it is to get a nugget of information and run with it."

When Mr. Sternham had first asked me about this, I had seriously thought it would never go anywhere. "Do you guys know how the press even found out about it?"

Herman and my father shrugged. "We just aren't sure how they found out. Not many people know. But it very well could've been someone with the FBI who tipped the *Enquirer* reporter off."

"What are we going to do?" I said.

"We"—my dad motioned around the room—"are on top of it and will get it under control. You," he said, turning back to me, "will just continue being the fabulous daughter that you are. Just like I told your mom, I'm not going anywhere, and this will be taken care of. You just keep focusing on Maya."

I sulked as I nodded, then headed up to my room. Focusing on Maya. Yeah, right. For the first time in my life, that was going to be easier said than done.

Chapter 28

I kicked off my Jimmy Choo spiked heels and rubbed my feet. *Memo to self*: Next time I have a show where I have to stand for a long time, wear more comfortable shoes.

"Hey, Maya," Ariel said, sticking her head in my office. I hoped she wasn't coming to offer me any fake condolences about the *Enquirer* article. I'd skipped out on school today just so I didn't have to deal with the drama, and everybody at work had something to say about that stupid article They acted all concerned, but I knew they were just being nosey.

All I knew was that my dad needed to get this situation cleared up ASAP, because I so did not need this drama. I was not about to be on the red carpet at the People's Choice Awards next month with this hanging over my head.

"Tamara needs to see you ASAP," Ariel said.

"For what?" I was so not in the mood for some meeting.

"I don't know," Ariel replied. "But she has some bigwigs in there with her, and it doesn't look good."

I didn't let my worry show because it was obvious Ariel was taking joy in something possibly being wrong, so I shrugged it off. Plus, I knew all she needed was a little dirt and she'd go running to tell other people on the staff. Since I was going to see Tamara, I was going to tell her that I wasn't feeling Ariel and that they needed to get me another assistant.

"You know I just passed by Ms. Collins's office. The suits don't look happy," Ariel added.

"Okay, thank you," I said.

"And Mr. Hart, the station's attorney, is in there."

"I said, thank you," I repeated, not bothering to hide my attitude.

"Umph, I was just letting you know." She wiggled her neck like some kind of ghetto drama queen before turning and stomping out of the office.

No, you're just being messy, I wanted to say. But now, I really was nervous. If the station's attorney, Mr. Hart, was there, that meant trouble. Tamara had told me from day one that if we saw him, it wasn't a good sign.

My stomach was in knots as I made the trek down the hall to her office. I assumed Mr. Hart was the stocky, blond man in the expensive suit. I recognized the other guy as the director of public relations. The room immediately fell silent when they noticed me in the doorway.

"Come on in, Maya," Tamara finally said. "Please have a seat." Her cold tone sent chills up my spine.

"Um, is everything okay?" I asked, not moving.

"Actually, it's not," she said, motioning to the empty chair in front of her desk. "Please, take a seat."

She waited for me to sit, then released a long sigh, before looking down at some papers on her desk. Mr. Hart and the guy with publicity still hadn't said a word. My producer, Dexter, who was sitting in the back, was eerily quiet as well.

"The story you ran about Daysia McKinney, the reality star, is proving problematic," Tamara began. "It appears the mug shot of Daysia was photoshopped to show her beat up, and the story was all wrong."

I looked at Tamara in confusion. "What do you mean, it was wrong?"

"Wrong, incorrect, a lie," Mr. Hart said. He didn't bother trying to hide his sarcasm.

When Tamara had first told me two days ago that there might be an issue with the story on Daysia, I had just given her all my source information. We had people complaining all the time about the stories I did. And everybody and their mama had threatened to sue me. I never paid them any attention, because most of the time, they were all just for show. I was so wrapped up in everything that was going on with me that I really hadn't thought there was a serious problem.

"There was an arrest record," I said. "That's what I reported."

"Yes, on air, that's what you said. But on the *Rumor Central* website, you posted the mug shot, and that's what Daysia's attorneys are saying was photoshopped. They say that she was not injured at all and that there never was an altercation, not to mention the erroneous information about some drug habit," Tamara said.

"And WSVV is ultimately responsible for anything on the *Rumor Central* website," Mr. Hart added.

"I didn't have anything to do with what went up on the website," I protested. "Jayla Cooper put that story up. I didn't know anything about it."

"So, you don't check the website?" the PR guy asked.

I turned up my nose at him. I had enough on my plate. Now I was supposed to be responsible for checking websites, too?

Mr. Hart spoke up. "Well, we've already spoken with Miss Cooper and Kelly. That's your assistant, right?" he asked Tamara, who nodded. "Jayla confirmed that you are the one who asked her to post the story on the website."

"Well, Jayla is a liar." I didn't think it was possible to hate Jayla any more than I already did. I was wrong.

"She showed us the email the request came from. Your email address," Mr. Hart said.

"I don't care what she showed you. Either someone has hacked into my email account again, or she's just flat-out lying."

Mr. Hart pushed his glasses up on his nose and still looked over the top of them at me. "Yes, Miss Cooper did inform us of your belief that someone has hacked into your email. She said you changed the password, and this particular email came *after* that change." He didn't seem like he was buying anything I was saying.

"That girl can't be trusted," I protested, giving Tamara the evil eye. If she had listened to me when I first tried to get rid of Jayla, this wouldn't be a problem. "I don't know why Jayla has it in for me, but she's trying to ruin my life."

Tamara picked up a stack of papers and dropped them back down on her desk. "So far, she's succeeding, because this is a million dollar lawsuit."

"A million dollars?" I exclaimed. "That's some bull. I was too through."

"Miss Morgan, did you properly vet the story before you went on the air with it?" Mr. Hart asked.

"No, that's why we have a research team. They're the ones who confirmed her arrest record." I didn't understand how all of this was turning into my fault.

"Yes, but did you get clearance from a manager before you ran with something that wasn't properly vetted?" he continued. He was talking to me like I was a child, and I so could not appreciate it. "Did you, Miss Morgan?"

"No, I mean, yeah. I got the tip right before I went on the air. We were short on time; our story had fallen through. What was I supposed to do?"

"You were supposed to run it by us," Tamara said.

"I called Dexter and told him what I had." I pointed back at Dexter. I expected him to jump in and say something, but he remained quiet.

"Did you run the stuff on the website by him?" Mr. Hart asked.

"I didn't have anything to do with what was on the site!" I yelled.

Tamara gave me a stern look, and I took a deep breath to calm down.

"So not only are we facing a libel suit for what was on the site, but our reputation is at stake because of that photoshopped picture," Mr. Hart said.

"Well, we need to be suing the person who gave me the information," I said. It had never dawned on me that the picture might not be real. I mean, seriously, who would go to all that trouble?

Mr. Hart frowned as he continued talking to me. "Yes, we checked the records and the number you put into the files for your source. It is the number for an area Pizza Hut."

"That's the number Ariel gave me. It was for Daysia McKinney's sister." I felt knots building in my stomach.

"Did you ever call it?" Tamara asked.

"Well, no. But Ariel actually talked to her. The sister just sent me an email with all the details."

"Yeah, we checked that out as well," Mr. Hart said, looking at his notes. "Turns out, Daysia McKinney doesn't have a sister."

I fell back in my seat. It felt like someone had hit me in my stomach with a hammer.

"Maya, this is bad. Real bad," Tamara said, shaking her head. Tamara had always been in my corner, but the look on her face told me that I was in this all by myself.

I couldn't believe this. I didn't know how, but somehow this was all tied to Jayla. I just knew it.

"Maya, I'm sorry, but we're going to have to suspend you until the investigation is complete." Tamara's voice was soft, and I could tell she was upset.

I looked at her in disbelief. "Suspend me? We just went

into syndication. How am I not gonna be on my own show? The people tune in to see me," I protested. "I'm the one digging up the dirt that makes this show."

"We don't want the dirt if it's wrong," Mr. Hart quipped.

"We will have Ariel Edwards fill in until this is all worked out," Tamara said, her voice calm. I know she was trying to keep me from getting any more worked up than I already was. "She's young, so we won't lose that core demographic."

The PR guy nodded. "And her demo tape was pretty good, so we think she'll be fine to fill in."

Ariel? My assistant? I knew she wanted my job but dang, she had actually given them her demo tape?

"You have got to be kidding me," I mumbled. Then it suddenly dawned on me that Ariel was the one who had brought me the Daysia McKinney story in the first place. What if she was the one who had set me up?

"I'm sorry, Maya," Tamara said. "It's just until we get all this worked out."

"*If* this all gets worked out," Mr. Hart corrected.

I could not believe I was about to lose my job over some bs. "Man, this is jacked up," I said, fighting back tears.

"Young lady, this is serious. I know you're young"—he eyed Tamara—"which is why I was completely against your hiring. But you will learn in this business that we cross all our t's and dot our i's to prevent this very thing from happening. Because if we don't, a lawsuit is the end result." He dropped his notepad in his briefcase, closed it, and stood.

"I need to check with the station owners and give them an update. I'll be in touch," Mr. Hart said, looking at Tamara. He glanced over at me. "Hopefully, there won't be any long-term damage done." Both Dexter and the PR guy followed him out.

"I don't believe this," I said, after they were gone. "Why am I getting suspended? I told you this was all Jayla. Or maybe even Ariel. But one of them set me up."

Tamara sighed heavily. She looked like the whole situation was as draining to her as it was to me. "Don't be ridiculous. Why would either of them try to set you up?"

"Because Jayla's a freak and Ariel wants my job."

"Ariel says all she did was take a phone call and pass the info on to you."

"*If* there even was a phone call. She might have made the whole thing up," I snapped.

"But, at the end of the day, it's your job to verify information you air on your show, or at least make sure it gets verified. It's not Ariel's job. When you go on the air, it's your name on the line. And besides, this isn't some type of plot. Dexter saw her tape and told me about it. She never asked me to let her fill in. I went to her."

Whatever. Tamara could play the fool if she wanted, but one of those girls was behind this.

"Why isn't Jayla getting in trouble, too? She's the one who posted the story on the website."

"Yes, but she said it was at your request."

"I keep telling you guys, she's a freakin' liar!"

Tamara let out a long, heavy sigh.

"Well, regardless, Jayla's been suspended as well."

"She doesn't need to be suspended. She needs to be fired!" I exclaimed. "She's the one behind all of this. And if she'd been fired back when I first requested it, none of this would be happening."

Tamara was quiet. I expected her to protest, but all she said was, "Bring me some proof, and we can permanently get rid of her."

I stopped ranting and stared at her. "So you believe me?"

"I know you, Maya. Been knowing you for years. You're a lot of things, but you're not just going to put something blatantly false out there. And I agree; we didn't start having these problems until Jayla came on board. And for all the good she's done promoting your career, it doesn't do any good if there's no career to promote."

"Why does she just get suspended? I want her gone."

"Okay."

"Okay?"

"Okay," Tamara repeated. "I'll find a way to get her out."

That was music to my ears. I almost reminded Tamara of how just a few days ago she had told me that wasn't possible, but I decided to count my blessings.

Firing was the first step, but I wouldn't stop there. I wouldn't be happy until Jayla paid for the havoc she was causing in my life.

Chapter 29

I could not lose my job. I *would* not lose my job—especially over some mess I didn't even do. I kept telling myself that as I made my way back to my office. Several people were looking at me and, I'm sure, trying to figure out what was going on.

I had just made it back to my office when Ariel came in.

"Is everything okay?" she asked.

I was trying my best to fight back tears and if I opened my mouth, I was sure my voice would crack, so I just nodded. Besides, I was beginning to think she wasn't as innocent as she tried to make out.

"Are you sure? Is this about Daysia McKinney? I heard she was upset about her story."

I froze. No, this chick didn't have the audacity to bring up a story she gave me—probably to set me up.

"Let me ask you a question. Did you know the story was fake? Did you set it all up?"

She looked appalled. "Me? Of course, not. I'm just as shocked by all of this as you."

I studied her for a minute. Finally, I said, "Whatever." I knew there was a reason I didn't trust her. And even if she hadn't known the story was fake, you can't tell me she wasn't glad I was in trouble because of it.

"So, do you need anything?" She looked around the office. "You need my help with anything?"

"I'm fine. Now excuse me, please." I walked past her and started gathering a few things off my desk.

She actually stood there staring at me. "Can I ask, I mean, rumor has it that you're being suspended. Is that true?"

My mouth dropped open. How in the world did these people know this already?

Ariel must have read the look on my face, because she shrugged and said, "You work for a gossip show. People gossip."

I tried to wave her comment off like it was no big deal. "It's all a big misunderstanding anyway, so it's seriously nothing for people to be talking about."

"You're not going to get fired or anything, are you?" She tried to look at me with puppy-dog eyes, like she was really concerned. Even though she'd apologized after our big blowup, I could tell she would never really like me, and the feeling was definitely mutual.

"No, I'm not getting fired." I turned to her and smirked. "But don't worry, I hear you're going to get your big break."

"What is that supposed to mean?"

"Oh, don't act like you don't know. Tamara told me that you'd be filling in."

Her eyes shifted, and she shrugged like she wasn't fazed. As hard as she'd been sweating me, I know she wanted to turn backflips at the opportunity, so I don't even know why she was trying to front. "Well, I didn't know if it was a done deal or not. Ms. Collins just asked me, and of course, I said yes. But she told me it was just temporary."

"Yeah, *it is*," I said matter-of-factly. Ariel didn't need to get it twisted. There wouldn't be but one diva in this joint.

"Well, if you need anything, you just let me know," Ariel said with the fakest smile I'd ever seen.

I'm sure she was taking great pleasure in this. "Just don't get too comfortable." I snatched my purse and my bag. "It *is* only temporary." I pushed past her and strutted out of the room.

Chapter 30

After a good overnight cry, I pulled myself together. I might be down, but it wouldn't be for long. I was determined that I wasn't going out like that.

I was on a mission to get some answers. That's why I was sitting here, enduring this geek-of-the-week salivating at the sight of me.

"I'm sorry for staring," he said, pushing his bifocals up on his nose. Alvin Hall actually wasn't bad looking. He had smooth skin, strong features, a tall build, and black, wavy hair. But he definitely needed a lot of work. I wanted to give him the number to a good Lasik surgeon, because those Coke-bottle glasses were so not the business. But since I needed something from him, I just smiled.

"It's okay," I replied, even though his staring was creeping me out.

"I'm just a little starstruck. I can't believe Maya Morgan is sitting in my bedroom," he said excitedly.

I couldn't believe it either, I thought, as I looked around at the dark room covered with computer equipment, comic books, and gaming stuff. Marvel comics and superhero

posters hung on the walls. Alvin's little twin bed even had a
Marvel comforter. Talk about whack. I'd never seen a grown
man with a bedroom like this, and I still couldn't believe I
was here. Oh, don't get it wrong. I wasn't here for *that*.
Kennedi had a friend who said if I needed to get to the bottom of any type of hacking or computer questions, Alvin
here was the man for the job. I'd wanted him to meet me
somewhere else, but Kennedi said he rarely left his room. He
even took his college courses online. So, I had to take what I
could get.

"So, do you think you'll be able to find out where the
emails are coming from?" I said, trying to direct his attention
back to his computer. I'd filled him in on everything I'd been
going through. He hadn't seemed surprised, saying he saw
this type of thing all the time. "I mean, I'm almost sure I
know who hacked my account, but I need some proof."

"Oh, yeah," Alvin said with enthusiasm. "That's an easy
one."

If it's so easy, can you give me an answer? I wanted to say. Instead, I smiled and said "Great."

"First, I have to scan your network to determine if it is
vulnerable to attacks. They most likely gained entry through
remote access, but you may have some open ports or even a
Trojan horse, which sets up a back door for optimum security
breach," he said.

Blank stare. He might as well have been speaking Swahili.

"Yeah, ummm, can you say that in English?"

He looked at me crazy. "That *was* English." I just stared at
him. Was anyone really this dumb? Then, he smiled and said,
"Ooooh, my bad. You didn't mean that literally." He released
the corniest laugh I'd ever heard. "Basically, it means that
someone has hacked into your computer from somewhere
else."

"How is that even possible?"

"Have you ever given your Wi-Fi password to anyone else?"

"Yeah," I said, remembering when Jayla had come over to set up my system.

He shook his head. "What about the password to your email accounts?"

"Yeah, to the girl who did my social media, but that's it."

"Bad move," he said, shaking his head some more.

"I changed all my passwords after we fell out, but it looks like she's still accessing my account."

"Do you leave your computer screen open?"

I didn't know what that had to do with anything. "Yeah, I do. Why?"

"Well, someone can hack in through your Wi-Fi that way, too, especially if they can figure out your password. What's your email address?"

I gave it to him, and he punched the keys. "What's your password at home for your Wi-Fi?"

"Password."

"Yeah, what's your password?"

"My password is *password*. I use it for my Wi-Fi and my email. I changed the email password but not the Wi-Fi. I didn't know I needed to change that one."

He stopped typing and stared at me like I was the stupidest person on the planet. "Really? Did you know that on the list of top ten passwords, *password* is number one?"

I looked at him like why would I know that. But I just shook my head and said, "Sorry, no."

He sighed. "Okay, what did you change your email password to?"

I almost didn't want to answer. I knew I was using something easy, but that's because I was super busy, and I did not have time to be remembering a whole bunch of stuff. Finally, I said, "123456."

He actually laughed. "That's number two on the list." He continued tapping on the keyboard. "You have to be original." He pushed the glasses up again. I wanted to tell him to *originally* get some glasses that fit. But, I kept my mouth closed and let him keep talking. He leaned back and turned to me. "The best thing is a combination of letters and numbers. Preferably something that's not easily discernible," he said casually. "And don't give your password to anyone, because once you do he or she can go in and set up keystroke logs or some other type of method to continue getting in."

"Okay." I pointed to the computer screen. "But can we finish?"

He turned back to the computer, tapped a few more keys, and a few minutes later, he said, "Ta-da! I'm in your laptop."

I frowned. "What do you mean you're in my laptop?"

He turned the screen toward me, and I saw "You are now accessing Maya's laptop."

"What? My laptop is at home, sitting on my desk."

"Did you leave it logged on to the Internet?"

I shrugged. "Probably."

"Then you're vulnerable." He said this like it was a no-brainer. He tapped feverishly on the keys like he was on a mission. "Yep. That's exactly what happened. I just accessed it remotely, so now, since your password is stored, I can just go in and send emails to whomever I want. It looks like that's what your hacker did. If I wanted, I could even go change your password so you couldn't get back in."

I couldn't believe what he was saying. "So, someone can get into my computer without having the actual computer?" I asked.

"Yep."

"And what do they do once they get in?"

"Anything they want. They can access all your files, your pictures, your documents, your email account." He touched the screen. "And since you're on a shared network, I can access all of your parents' stuff, too."

"That's how she did it," I mumbled. "Can you tell where it was accessed from, I mean, who actually did it?"

"Sure." He turned the computer screen back toward him, punched a few more keys, then said, "Looks like someone at this IP Address has been having a ball on your computer." He pointed to a long number that popped up on his screen. "GPS won't pinpoint the exact address," he said peering at the screen. "But the IP address is coming from this vicinity."

He again turned the computer to face me. A Google map filled his screen. He zoomed in—and I recognized Jayla's neighborhood immediately.

"Just wow," I said.

"Here's the list of times this person has accessed your computer," Alvin said, pointing to the side of the screen. I was dumbfounded at the long list of times. She was using my computer more than me.

"I can't believe she did this," I said to myself.

"You know this person?"

"Yeah, I think I do. No, I'm sure I do."

"You must've really done something to her to make her mad. Either that or she's some kind of stalker."

"I have no idea. All I know is I haven't done anything to her. Yet." I shook my head. This was just so freakin' unbelievable. "Can I have her arrested?"

Alvin looked at me sadly. "Sorry, I'm no cop, but I think since she didn't take any money, you're not going to have much luck with the cops."

I buried my face in my hands, trying to think how I was going to handle this.

"Well, do you want me to go in and secure your systems?" Alvin finally asked.

I thought about it. Of course, I didn't want this trick in

my accounts anymore, but I wasn't sure I was ready to let Jayla know I was on to her. I had to come up with a plan to bust her.

I sat up and looked at him. "Not yet. But I'll definitely be back in touch in a couple of days."

"No problem. Just let me know and I'll get you set up so that the CIA can't even hack into your computer," he said.

I scooted back from the computer. "Thanks so much, Alvin. You don't know what a help you've been."

Alvin smiled, and, for the first time, I noticed that he had the cutest dimples.

"No problem. Glad to help." He got up and walked me out. "Hey, we can go through here," he said, pointing to the side door.

I followed him and had to stop when I noticed what was sitting in his garage. "Is that a Corvette?"

He grinned proudly. "Yep. That's my baby. It's a classic. 1953 Corvette. Only three of them made. Like it?"

"Wow. That car has to be worth a lot."

"Six-hundred thirty-seven thousand to be exact." He shrugged. "But it's priceless to me."

Dang, who would've ever thought Alvin was rocking something like that. He must have read my expression, because he said, "Yeah, I had a little computer invention I sold, and this car was my gift to myself."

I smiled. I wasn't knocking him, but I could've thought of a whole bunch of other things he could've bought, like Lasik eye surgery, a new wardrobe. . . .

"Well, if you need anything else, you just let me know," he said when we reached my car.

"I will. Thanks again."

He paused, then said with a smile, "Ummm, well, Marcus said that you'd give me a kiss if I helped you out."

"Umm, yeah, Marcus lied." The dejected look on his face

actually made me feel bad. So I leaned in and pecked him on the cheek. "That's all you get."

"That's all? You sure?"

"Yep. I'm sure."

He smiled. "You can't blame a guy for trying."

"No, you can't, and thanks for your help. I won't forget this."

He opened my door, and I climbed in my car. I waved once again, grateful that Kennedi had turned me on to Marcus, who had turned me on to Alvin, because Alvin had put me on just the path I needed to be on to bring Jayla Cooper down.

Chapter 31

I didn't recognize the 310 number that was blaring across my phone. I was so not in the mood to be dealing with people, but 310 was Los Angeles, so it might be one of my celebrity contacts. I might be temporarily out of pocket, but I still needed to keep working for when I did get back on air. Besides, I was waiting on Kennedi to call me back so I could tell her what Alvin had told me. Still, I went ahead and pushed the Talk button.

"You've got Maya," I said.

"Hey, Maya." I didn't immediately recognize the voice until I heard that distinctive laugh of my childhood friend. "That's real cute, girl. Real cute."

"Hey, Kelis," I replied. "Long time no talk to. What's up?" Kelis was a singer who had made a name for herself as one-third of the group, Dynasty. She was now experiencing success as a solo artist. We'd known each other since we were in elementary school, and even though she was always on the road, we kept in touch.

"Shoot, I need to be asking you that," Kelis replied. "You are blowing up, *chica!*"

"I'm trying, but girl, right now, I'm just dealing with

some major drama." I pushed through the clothes on my closet rack, trying to find something to wear to school tomorrow. When I had trouble finding an outfit, I knew I was off my game.

"Yeah, that's why I was calling. Somebody named Ariel called to introduce herself to me and told me she was taking your place and if I had any exclusive dirt or tips I wanted to talk about, you'd suggested that I now bring them to her."

That stopped me cold. "Shut the front door!" So this chick had the nerve to try and steal my job *and* my contacts?

"Yep. It was really weird," Kelis said. "I mean who does that?"

"Some low-life trick who's trying to get your job but doesn't have what it takes to succeed on her own," I replied.

"Well, you know me. I don't get down like that, so I straight asked her how she got my number."

"What did she say?" I asked, even though I knew the answer.

"She said from your address book."

I shook my head. I should've known keeping my digital address book on my work computer wasn't a good idea. But Ariel had a lot of nerve.

"So, like for real, what is the deal? What is she talking about, taking your place?"

"Girl, some drama with Daysia McKinney jumped off."

"The reality star?"

"Yeah, her. She got arrested recently, and someone sent me a mug shot that we aired, only the picture was photoshopped, some of the info was wrong, and I got in all kinds of trouble at work."

"Wow. Who would do that? This Ariel chick?"

"I have no idea. I'm thinking it's this girl we hired to do my social media. But you can best believe I'm going to find out."

"Dang, you've got your hands full. But look here; I was

also calling because I'm having a birthday party there on Saturday. The label is sponsoring it."

Kelis was with Bad Boy Records, and I'd been to a couple of their parties over the years. Talk about going all-out.

"Anyway, I know you got a lot going on, but that may be all the more reason why you need to come out. Have a good time, try to put your troubles behind you—at least for the night."

I thought about what she was saying. That sounded like a good idea. "You know what, I probably could use a good party right now. Can I bring Kennedi?" I asked.

"Yeah, the more the merrier. I haven't seen Kennedi in years, so it'll be good to catch up. I'm going to leave your VIP tickets at the front."

I hesitated. "Ummm, can I pick those tickets up ahead of time?"

Kelis chuckled and said, "Yeah, I heard about that J. Love drama, but I don't think they'll be ready for pickup before the party starts. But I'll have my assistant call and give you the number so you can verify that your name is on the list before you roll out to the party. How's that?"

"That works." I finally laughed. "Thanks, Kelis. It's just, after the last few weeks I have had, I'd rather play it safe, because if one more thing happens to me, it might just send me over the edge." We were laughing, but I really and truly meant that.

Chapter 32

"**I** told you, I told you, I told you!" Kennedi's high-pitched voice belted over the phone. She'd finally called me back on ooVoo after I got off the phone with Kelis. I filled her in on the party, which she was all too excited about, then, I replayed as much of Alvin's conversation as I could recall. She hadn't even addressed the whole hacking thing. She just kept going on and on about how she had tried to tell me Jayla was foul.

"I knew that chick was no good," Kennedi continued.

"Well, you should've told me that she was a psycho stalker, and I might have listened," I said as I lay back on my bed.

"No, you wouldn't have," Kennedi replied. "And I did tell you. From the stuff you told me, the girl just seemed creepy. Come to think of it, you have a knack for attracting those types." She laughed.

"This isn't funny, Kennedi." I was still trying to process everything Alvin had told me, especially the fact that unless she had stolen some of my money, there was probably nothing the cops would do.

"Okay, you're right. It isn't funny. It's sad. And actually pretty scary that someone can get in your stuff just like that."

I let out a long sigh. I should've known this was too good to be true. And to think, I'd thought Jayla was the best thing ever. "I don't know why this girl is trying to take over my life."

"I guess she wants your life or something, or maybe she has some kind of personal beef. The good thing is you're onto her. How are you gonna bust her?"

"I have no idea. It's not like I can get close to her. She doesn't trust me or anyone I know." I paused, thinking. "Except for Shay," I said, recalling how they were laughing it up the other day.

"Oh, and Shay probably hates you just as much as she does," Kennedi said.

"You're right about that." I began pacing back and forth across my bedroom. I had to figure this out. "I just hate that Alvin said unless she's trying to get money or do stuff in my name, there's no crime," I said.

"Alvin is a computer nerd, not a cop. What does he know? And, I'm sorry, impersonating someone is a crime. And didn't you prove all the stuff was coming from her IP address?"

"We think it's her, but like Alvin said, you can't prove that it was actually her who was sending all that stuff from my accounts. She can say anyone used her computer, and she could just keep harassing me."

"Well, can't you confirm what her ESP address is?"

"IP address," I corrected.

"So now you're Bill Gates?"

I finally laughed as I plopped back down on my bed. "Nah, just frustrated. But no, there's no way I can confirm her IP address, not without access to her computer."

"That's jacked up. So what are you going to do?"

"Jayla may think she has one-upped me, but she doesn't know me at all." I'd been thinking about how I could bust her, and I didn't know, but I was definitely going to figure out something.

"You need to let someone else handle this. Remember, you tried to set up Valerie, and you almost ended up dead." Kennedi let out a long sigh. "Okay, I have an idea, but you might not like it."

"At this point, I will listen to anything."

"Okay, you said if you can confirm her address, you can pretty much prove the emails are coming from her. That means if you could just get access to her computer, then you would have the proof you need."

"Oh, is that all I need to do?" I said sarcastically. "Let me call Jayla right now and see if she'll let me come over and use her laptop."

"Look, smart alec, I'm trying to help you out."

I rubbed my temple. "Sorry. This is all too much for my brain to process. I want to be worried about designer clothes and shoes and what my next big story will be, not all this nerd computer stuff."

"Well, I promise you that girl isn't going to stop unless you stop her." Kennedi hesitated. "And all you need is for Shay to help you," she quickly added.

"Oh, now I know you're crazy for real."

"Seriously, you just have to make up with Shay and get her to help you since you said Jayla doesn't trust any of you guys but Shay."

"Oh, like that's gonna happen."

"Oh, you have to *make* it happen. Apologize—"

I cut her off. "I'm not apologizing to her."

"Maya, you need to apologize. And you know that's saying a lot coming from me, because I don't like any of those chicks. But you know you were wrong for how all of that went down. I'm not mad at you for how everything went down. You were taking care of business. But it was still jacked up. So apologize."

"I apologized once." I rolled my eyes. There had to be another way.

"Well, apologize again. And tell her again how you didn't post that mess about her dad. Then, ask for her help."

"That plan sounds whack."

"Well, I don't know what else to tell you. That's all I got. You do what you want to do."

What I wanted was for all of this to go away. But since that wasn't happening, I also wanted to know why in the world Jayla Cooper had it out for me so bad.

"Look, can we talk about more pleasant things? Like this party. What are you wearing?" I asked.

"I have no idea."

I pulled myself up and made my way over to my large walk-in closet and glanced around. My eyes settled on a Versace party dress that I hadn't worn, but had bought just for a big party like this. "Oh, remember that Versace dress I was telling you about?"

"Yeah, the one you bought at that boutique downtown? Let me see it."

I held the dress up to my phone.

"Ooooh, yeah, that's the business."

"Cool, then, I'll wear this." I hung the dress back up.

"Look, I know you got a lot going on, but deal with it, and this weekend, let it go, a'ight? We're just gonna have a good time."

I nodded, said good-bye, and hung up. I heard what Kennedi was saying. She just didn't understand that was a lot easier said than done.

Chapter 33

I was so ready to get my party on. I wanted to forget the stress that had become my life and just party—hard. Because I was in Miami's "in" crowd, I was already invited to the top Miami parties, but since I'd become host of *Rumor Central*, I'd stepped up my party game. Even though, most of the time, I wasn't even old enough to get into the club, I was the celebrity attraction. I loved it, but tonight I was just looking forward to hanging out with my girls and enjoying myself.

Tonight, Kennedi was rolling solo with me. Sheridan's mom was in town, so they had to do the family thing. Needless to say, she was too through about having to miss the party, but I told her we'd take a lot of pictures. Kennedi and I both looked fab. She had on a fuchsia silk off-the-shoulder top and some sequined boy shorts. Of course, both of us were rocking Louboutins, which just set our outfits off.

I'd arranged for a driver drop us off so that I didn't have to fool with parking. I knew it was going to be bananas at the place where the party was being held. We rolled up to the event in style. The driver opened our door, and we stepped out looking like the divas that we were.

"Are you sure we're not going to have any problems?" Kennedi asked. "Because I can't handle a scene like last time."

"Would you chill?" I snapped. "Kelis told me to call her if there were any problems."

"I thought you were going to get the passes ahead of time?"

"I tried, but Kelis said I couldn't. But don't worry. I just talked to her before we left. She said everything's good."

"Okay, it better be, or else you're gonna be rolling to parties by yourself from now on," Kennedi playfully threatened.

We strutted up the sidewalk to the bouncer. Once again, there was a long line of folks. This time, we were smart enough to ignore those people who were grumbling and not get into it with anyone.

"Hi, I'm Maya Morgan," I told the bouncer. "I'm on the VIP list."

He scanned his clipboard, then frowned. "You've already checked in."

I could immediately feel Kennedi's whole body tense up.

"No, obviously, I haven't checked in since I'm standing right here," I replied with a strained smile. Kennedi was glancing around nervously to see if anyone was watching us. The whole line of people had their eyes glued on us.

The bouncer looked at his list again, shook his head, then said, "You got some ID on you?"

I inhaled, trying not to freak out, reached in my clutch, then pulled out my license and handed it to him.

He studied it, then looked back at his list. "Sorry, my bad," he said, handing the license back to me. "I must've crossed off the wrong name." He removed the rope and stepped to the side to let us pass. "Have a good time."

"Thank you," I said. Kennedi breathed a huge sigh of relief. Quiet as it's kept, so did I.

"My pleasure, beautiful ladies," the bouncer said as we passed him.

"Girrrrl, I thought we were about to have a repeat," Kennedi said.

"I told you it wasn't going down like that."

Inside the dark club, the music was thumping. The walls vibrated from the sounds of the bass. The dance floor was packed, and people were lined up wall-to-wall. A Bad Boy banner hung across the stage, and a giant poster of Kelis sat on the edge of the stage.

I felt my phone vibrate and looked down to see a text message from Kelis.

Look up! VIP is up here

I glanced up and saw Kelis waving. We pushed through all the people and finally made our way upstairs to the roped-off private area.

"Hey, Kelis," I said, hugging her. "You're looking tight as always."

She did a little twirl; I don't even see how it was possible in that skin-tight catsuit. Only Kelis could make a catsuit look fly. "You know how I do it."

"Hey, girl. Happy birthday," Kennedi said, reaching out to hug her.

"K-K, waaaazzzz up!" They hugged, and Kelis pulled back. "Girl, I haven't seen you in forever. You were still rocking those colored braces last time I saw you."

Kennedi flashed her perfect smile. "And they all paid off, baby!"

Kelis turned back to me. "Maya, girl, you look hot! But ummm, wow . . ." She stopped and fought back a giggle.

What was that about? "Why you say it like that?" I asked.

"I'm just wondering, I mean, I can't believe the fashion diva is shopping off-the-rack now?"

"Kelis, what in the world are you talking about?"

"Off-the-rack." She pointed to my dress. "I just assumed that's where your dress came from."

"Are you crazy? Why would you assume that?" I exclaimed. Like most of my stuff, this Versace was an original. I bought off-the-rack every now and then, but I definitely wouldn't be caught dead at a party wearing something I'd bought in some department store. "This is an original Versace."

Kelis sipped her drink and looked at me slyly. "Oh, okay. I just thought maybe there was a sale at Macy's or something on the dress."

"Okay, you're not making sense." I asked.

She pulled me by my arm toward the end of the balcony, then scanned the crowd below. Finally, she said, "There," pointing to some chick posted up against the wall. "Your *original* dress."

I saw the girl she was talking about, and I wanted to die. This was exactly why I ordered originals of everything from this exclusive boutique that my mom got most of her stuff from. Oh, the owner was definitely going to hear from me!

"You have got to be freakin' kidding me," I mumbled.

Kennedi, who had come up next to me and was looking over the balcony as well, was equally horrified.

"The only reason I noticed it was because she tried to get up here, and I remembered saying her dress was cute."

"Oh my God, Maya," Kennedi said. "What are you gonna do?" The girl's back was to us, but there was no mistaking it; that was my dress.

"I cannot be up in this party with this girl wearing the same dress as me," I said.

"We can leave," Kennedi said. I could tell that was the last thing she wanted to do, but that just showed she was truly my girl if she was willing to do that.

"I'm not leaving," I said. "This no-name chick can go. She's a nobody."

"How do you know she's a nobody?" Kennedi said.

"If she were somebody, she'd be in the VIP section," I replied. "I'm about to go offer her some money to go home."

Kelis shook her head. "I ain't even mad at you, girl. Do you." She noticed someone waving from the other side of the room and said, "I'll be right back. There's my sister."

I didn't even pay Kelis any attention as she walked off. My eyes were focused squarely on the chick rocking my Versace original.

"I'm going down there," I said.

Kennedi stopped me just as I was turning away. "Maya, it's a bunch of people here. No one is going to see you."

"Yeah, it's a bunch of press here, too. I'm not about to be in the 'Who Wore It Better' section of *People* Magazine."

Kennedi sighed. "You can't go down there, because people will start snapping pictures." She looked around like she was trying to figure out what to do. "I'm not your freakin' assistant, but desperate times call for desperate measures, so I'll go talk to her."

I watched as Kennedi went down and talked to the girl. I could only see the girl from the back, and I could barely make out Kennedi's expression, but I could tell by the way she was bobbing and waving her arms that she wasn't too happy.

I knew I was right when she came stomping back up to the VIP area.

"This chick is crazy!" she said. "First, she said she wasn't going anywhere. Then she said if you wanted her to leave, you needed to come tell her yourself."

"What?"

"I don't know." Kennedi shook her head. "I don't know if she wants to meet you or what?"

"And you offered her some money?"

Kennedi nodded. "Yep. But I'm here to have a good time. I'm not about to get into it with one of your deranged fans."

"Fine. Whatever." I glanced down and saw the flash from some cameras snapping, meaning paparazzi was here in full effect. "Okay, can you do me this one last favor?"

Kennedi rolled her eyes.

"Please? Just go tell her to come on up. I'll sign an autograph or whatever she wants to get her out of here."

Kennedi didn't move.

"Please? This is the last thing I'll ask."

"You're lucky you're my girl," Kennedi said as she stomped back downstairs.

No way would I be able to enjoy myself with this girl here in my dress. I felt a flutter of relief when Kennedi and the girl disappeared up the back entrance that would lead them upstairs.

"You handle her from here," Kennedi said as she passed me and headed to the bar.

"Where is she?" I asked.

Kennedi turned around. "She was right behind me."

And then, from the stairwell, she emerged. "You wanted to see me?"

Oh. My. God. "Are you freakin' kidding me?"

My mind immediately went back to the bouncer's saying I'd already checked in.

"Are you impersonating me? How did you know what I was going to be wearing?" I asked in disbelief. I hadn't known what I would be wearing until I showed Kennedi on ooVoo. But I had been on my phone. Could she have hacked that, too? Maybe she had a spy camera in my house. "What kind of freak are you?"

Jayla just stood there, smirking, and I swear, if people hadn't been standing around watching us, I would've hauled off and knocked the mess out of her.

"Why are you dressed like me?" Still silence. "Answer me, you freak!" I yelled.

"Don't they say imitation is flattery or something like that?"

Okay, forget who was watching. I was about to beat this trick down. "You b—"

"Whoaaaa," Kelis said, stepping in and pushing me back. "Maya, what are you doing?" she frantically said.

"I'm about to beat this freak right here down for following me around, dressing like me. . . ." I shouted as I bucked toward Jayla.

"Taking your man, did you forget that part?" Jayla laughed, and I snapped, lunging in her direction.

By that point, security was over and stopped me before my fist connected with her eye.

"What is your problem, you deranged lunatic?" I yelled as the security guard pulled me back.

"Maya, chill!" Kelis said, actually pushing me back. "There will be no fighting at my birthday party."

"Yeah, Maya," Jayla replied, all cocky. "This is a classy affair."

Kelis spun around and glared at Jayla. "I'm gonna have to ask you to leave."

Jayla put her hands on her hips. "You can't make me leave."

"I can make you do anything I want since it's my party." Kelis stepped closer, pointing her index finger directly in Jayla's face. "So I'm gonna need you to roll up on out of here. Or I will turn my girl loose, and both of us will beat you down—with class."

"Whatever," Jayla said, although she wasn't as cocky as she had been a few minutes ago.

"I know you don't have a life of your own, but go find someone else to stalk. Freak," I added. I couldn't believe her.

Jayla headed back to the stairs, but then stopped and spun around. "Boo, it's only just beginning. Believe that."

The bouncer took her arm and pushed her toward the stairs. "Come on, ma'am."

Jayla snatched her arm away. "I'm leaving."

"Who is that chick?" Kelis asked in disbelief.

"She used to work for me. And now, apparently, she wants my life."

"Dang, her too? What in the world have you been doing to these people?"

I stood there, fuming. Kelis just didn't know, but that was the million dollar question, because I had no idea what I'd done to Jayla Cooper.

Chapter 34

I don't know how my dream life turned into a nightmare. I didn't know how, but I did know why. Jayla Cooper.

My daddy's security team had found out how the *Enquirer* had gotten their story. It had come in an email tip to Mr. Sternham, sent on the same day that they received the J. Love story. It hadn't come from my email address, but it was sent at the same time by an email address that no longer existed. As soon as my dad told me that, I knew that Jayla had to be involved. Alvin said she could access my parents' computer, so she must have found out about the money laundering charges and tipped off that reporter when she sent the J. Love story.

I didn't say anything to my dad—yet—because I still couldn't prove it was Jayla. Besides, it was my fault this chick was in our lives, so I needed to figure out how to clean it up. Since I wasn't about to ask Shay for help, I needed to do something. That's why I was sitting here in Starbucks, searching the web on how to track down hackers. It was a shame that Jayla had me too scared to do this at home. Just that thought made me even angrier.

After I had spent a while browsing, my cell phone rang.

"Hi, Maya, it's Alvin," he said after I answered.

"Hey, Alvin," I said.

"I was just calling to check on you. I know everything you're going through has you bummed out, and I just wanted to make sure you were okay."

"I'm as okay as I can be with all that's going on."

"I hate that you're going through this. I know what a hassle something like this can be."

"Yeah, well, I just wanted to say thank you for believing me and not thinking I was some kind of freak."

"Oh, come on, Maya. You know you made all that up because you wanted to come hang out with me."

I was about to get offended, but then he laughed. He actually made me smile for the first time that day.

"I'm sure you're a blast to hang out with, but I'm still trying to get to the bottom of everything. That's what I'm doing now. I'm in Starbucks now doing some research on how to catch this girl." I leaned back in my chair and closed my eyes. "This stuff has taken over my life."

"Well, that's actually what I was calling about. Did you find anything else out?" he asked.

"No. I just don't understand how she's still accessing my stuff when I changed all the passwords. Yesterday, she showed up at a party wearing the same dress I had on. But I was on my phone when I showed my friend the dress. So either she hacked my phone, too, or she has cameras in my house. It's driving me crazy."

He hesitated like he was thinking. "You said you *showed* your friend the dress. Were you on Tango or something?" he asked.

"OoVoo."

"Which is still online. All she has to do is log in to your ooVoo account, and she can watch your conversations."

I wanted to scream. Right there, in Starbucks, let out the loudest scream I'd ever screamed.

"I can't believe this," I cried. That's how she had known about J. Love and everything else. She had seen me on ooVoo with Kennedi! This was both creepy and disgusting.

"Yeah, it's like I said; once you leave the door open, your hacker has access to everything you do online. She can see it all through remote access. That's why people keep getting emails that you didn't send. They are coming from your email address, but it's because she's logging in as you. She can see video chats, emails, photos, everything. She might also have password Decryptor," he continued. "Anything you change the password to, she can still see."

"This is crazy."

"When you don't protect your online presence, it's like leaving open the front door to your house and just letting someone walk in. And now, she knows her way around, and you might get a different lock, but she still knows how to get in."

"That's messed up. So what can I do?"

"You can let her know you're onto her, and that may stop her, but it won't do anything about the damage that's already done."

"Are you sure I can't take this to the police?"

"You can, but honestly, it's a cyber crime and will most likely go to the bottom of their list, because they'll say there's no damage done."

"No damage done?"

"Trust me, I know the damage that can be done on the Internet; but to them, cyber crimes that don't involve any money just don't get a high priority. They'll think the fact that she's hacking your email or hijacking your computer is petty."

I just didn't understand how anyone could think what I was going through was petty.

"I have a friend at the police station who I can call for you. He works in the cyber-crimes division. Maybe he can give us some more insight on what to do," Alvin said.

"Every little bit helps. I would actually appreciate your looking into this," I replied.

"Maya, if you can figure out a way to gain access to her laptop, you can go to What'sMyIPAddress.com, and it'll tell you what the address is for that computer. That's all you need as proof. And with proof you can prosecute."

"Yeah, my best friend suggested that, too," I said. "But there's no way I can get near her computer."

"Do you know anyone who can?"

My mind raced back to Shay. "I do, but we fell out."

"Now may be the time to make up."

Why did all roads to busting Jayla keep coming back to Shay? It was looking more and more like I was going to have to suck it up and apologize to Shay face-to-face and pray that she helped me.

"Or, I can just hack your hacker back for you," Alvin said.

I smiled, flattered that he would even offer to do something like that.

"Oh, I want to hack her all right. But not in cyberspace. I want to hack her upside her head."

He laughed. "Okay, but look, you said you were working on a research paper. Shoot, all this research you're doing right now, that's your paper right now."

I couldn't even focus on my paper right now, I was too upset.

"Thanks, that's an idea," I said, blowing him off. I quickly caught myself. I didn't need to be getting upset with him. "Thanks for all your help, Alvin."

"No problem. Now, you hang on to my number, and if I can be of any help, you just let me know." He paused. "And if you ever get lonely and need a date, I'll see if I can pencil you in."

"I'll keep that in mind." I couldn't help but smile as I hung up the phone.

Alvin was cool and all, but someone like me wouldn't be caught dead with someone like him. But I sure was thankful for all the information he was giving me, and hopefully, it would help me catch a crook.

Chapter 35

I don't think I'd ever been so nervous, especially because of some person. It wasn't Shay who actually scared me, but her dad. I prayed that he or her mother didn't answer the door.

I didn't even know if the story on the *Rumor Central* website about her parents had been true or not. (We did end up taking it down.) I just knew that I hadn't had anything to do with it. And I needed to convince Shay of that—then get her to help me.

I really hadn't wanted to come over here, but Kennedi was right; I needed to talk to Shay face-to-face. Sheridan had agreed and had reluctantly tagged along, and had even convinced Evian to come.

After I rang the doorbell a couple of times, the door was snatched open. Shay stood there, looking like some kind of ghetto princess in a Juicy Couture baby-doll T-shirt and some Daisy Duke shorts.

"You must have some kind of death wish," she said, glaring at me.

Sheridan stepped up first. She had felt like I should do this alone. I wasn't stupid, though. I had told her that if she didn't go, I didn't go. Shay's daddy was from the hood; I wasn't going to have his boys shoot me execution style with no witnesses. Then, Sheridan had decided Shay might listen even better if Evian was with us.

"Just chill before you go off. I think you need to hear Maya out," she said.

Shay looked at her like Sheridan was crazy. "There is nothing she can say that I want to hear."

I pushed Sheridan aside. "I know we have our beef," I began, "but I didn't do that. I wouldn't sell you out like that."

"Yeah, just like you wouldn't sell Evian out," Shay said, her voice full of sarcasm.

Evian raised an eyebrow like she agreed.

I glanced back at her. "I didn't sell Evian out. I sold her business out, but not *her.*"

"Can we just come in and talk?" Sheridan said.

"Are your parents here?" I asked.

Shay laughed, then turned up her lips. "Why? You can write about my parents, but you can't face them?"

"I didn't do that."

"Can you just let us in?" Sheridan repeated before Shay could get worked up.

"Fine," Shay said, stepping to the side.

We pushed past her. I was hesitant, because as much as I was trying to extend a peace offering, if she laid a hand on me, it was on.

Shay shut the door, and we followed her through the grand foyer, back into her den. She didn't offer us a seat, but we each took one anyway. There was an awkward silence for a minute before Sheridan said, "You know how Maya is. It took a lot for her to come here."

"Am I supposed to be impressed?" Shay said, raising an eyebrow to let us know that she was not moved.

I sat up. I wasn't going to let Sheridan fight my battles for me. I was going to say what I had to say, and if Shay couldn't deal with it, oh well.

"Look, Shay, I'm real sorry about the whole *Miami Divas* thing, but this, I had nothing to do with that story. If I did, I would own up to it," I said. "I'm not going to do something like that then pretend that I don't know anything about it. I own my stuff."

Evian cut her eyes at me. "She's right about that, Shay," she said, even though she was acting like it pained her to agree with me.

Shay looked like she was taking in what I said. "Then, if you didn't do it, how did it get on your website?"

"I think Jayla did it."

"Jayla? Who works with you?"

"Yep. Jayla Cooper who used to work for me."

"Why would she do it?"

"I don't know, but ever since she came on board, stuff like this has been happening. Something is going on with her. People are getting emails from my account that I didn't send. Stuff is being posted on the *Rumor Central* website that I had nothing to do with. And right now, I'm trying to prove it was her."

"Maybe someone else hacked into your account—*if* anyone even hacked into your account. Why are you assuming it's her? There's a lot of people who can't stand you," she said matter-of-factly.

"I just know it was Jayla. We think she's accessing my computer remotely."

Shay looked at me like I was making stuff up. "I never heard of anything like that."

"Me either. Until now," I said.

"So, why she'd do all of this?"

"Well, I don't know why the stuff was happening earlier. Now I think it's happening because we fired her, and it's like she's so mad that she's trying to take over my life."

Shay turned up her nose. "I don't know why she would want to do that."

I wasn't going to get into it with Shay, because I don't know, if the tables were turned, if I would believe her either. Even still, I was only going to give her a few more times to go off.

"So, I'm gonna ask again, why are you here?" Shay said. "What does this have to do with me? It doesn't change the fact that your stupid site put my parents on blast."

"We're here because I need your help," I managed to say.

Shay actually busted out laughing. "Ha! Isn't this karma? So what do you need my help for?"

"I need you to get close to Jayla. I'm trying to get to her computer," I said.

Shay took her time, leaning in and picking up her Coke, then taking a sip before saying, "And I'm the only person who can do that?"

I nodded.

"She knows about your beef with Maya," Sheridan said. "You're the only person who Jayla would trust."

Shay smiled. She was eating this up. "So, Maya needs me to save her behind?" Shay didn't bother waiting for an answer as she scooted to the edge of her seat. "Well, look here, if I'm the only way Maya can get out of this mess . . . Maya is so screwed!!" She busted out laughing again as she stood and walked out of the den and back toward the front of the house. We quietly followed her. I wasn't about to beg.

She held the front door open. "It'll be a cold day before I help that backstabber. As far as I'm concerned, anything Maya Morgan gets, she more than deserves!"

Sheridan stepped up. "Shay . . ."

Shay held up her hand to stop her. "Good-bye."

They could stay all they wanted, but I was out. Shay had shown her true colors, and as far as I was concerned, we didn't ever have to speak again.

Chapter 36

I finally sat down to try and figure out this research paper. Once again, I had waited to the last minute, although this time, I actually had a good reason. My life had become chaos.

I'd just opened my laptop when I noticed a text from Alvin.

Hey, Maya, it's Alvin. Call me ASAP.

I don't know why, but I felt a sense of urgency, and so I quickly dialed his number.

"Hey, Maya," he answered.

"Hey, Alvin, what's going on?"

"I talked to my friend in the cyber crime unit," he began. "It's like I suspected; if there's no money involved, meaning she's not trying to get your money, they're really not going to make it a priority."

"Yeah, you told me that, which is why I didn't go to the cops."

"That's actually not why I'm calling though. I gave my friend your name, because I wanted him to make a note of it in the system, and your name popped up—already in the system."

I frowned. What in the world was he talking about? "What do you mean, already in the system?"

Alvin paused like he was trying to figure out what to say. "Okay, I don't quite know how to say this."

"Just say it, Alvin." My head was throbbing, and I didn't have time to play guessing games.

"It looks like there's been a police report filed. Against you."

That made me sit straight up. "Against me? Saying what?"

"Yeah, Jayla Cooper filed a police report, saying that you've been harassing her. She's actually seeking a restraining order."

"You have got to be kidding me." I laughed. But I think it was so I wouldn't cry.

"I wish I was."

"*She* has a restraining order against *me?*"

"She doesn't actually have one yet. She's trying to get one. And it looks like in order to do that, she had to file this police report first."

"If this doesn't beat all. Why is she filing a report against me?" I got up and started pacing the floor in my bedroom. I needed to move, to do something to keep the anger inside me from building.

"The report just says you've been harassing her, making false claims."

"So, I couldn't even file a police report if I wanted to," I said.

"You could. But because she did it first, it could get messy."

I just could not believe the way all of this was unfolding. I found my mind racing back to when I first met Jayla. It had been all too convenient. Her being at the mall just as I was being attacked. Her being my number one fan. My bringing her on board at the station. Yeah, Jayla Cooper had definitely been setting me up.

"I'm sorry to have to tell you that," Alvin continued. "But I just wanted you to be aware. I know she's pushing your buttons, but she may be trying to provoke you, because if you hit or harass her, she could have you arrested."

"She could have me arrested. That is so messed up!" This was un-freaking-believable.

"Maya, I don't know what your plans are to bring the girl down, but you need to get that proof. You need to find out her IP address. My contact said that's all we need, and her police report will be thrown out, and you can press charges against her."

"I just don't need this. I finally sat down to try and figure out what to do for this stupid research paper due in a few days. Now I have the stress of this hanging over my head."

"What research paper?"

"For my English class," I replied. "We have to do an informative paper." I sighed. "And I have no idea what to do."

"Ummm, you've done more than enough research on your own situation. Why not do the paper on cyber crimes? Half your work is already done."

He was right about that. Alvin had come through again.

"That's a great idea." I heard the garage door open. "Hey, Alvin, thanks for calling me. My parents are coming in, so I'm going to need to go."

"Have you told them what's going on?" he asked.

"I hadn't, but maybe it's time."

"Okay, good luck. Talk to you soon."

I hung up just as my parents walked in the door with huge grins. They both were in business attire, which was unusual for my mom.

"Hey, sweet pea," my mom sang as they walked in.

"What are you in such a good mood for?" I asked.

She went to the cabinet and got out two wine glasses.

"Your dad and I are about to celebrate. Grab a Coke. You can join in."

"Celebrate what?" I asked.

My dad loosened his tie. "Try as they might, no one can bring down a Morgan," my dad said.

My mom walked over and poured both herself and my dad some wine that she'd just gotten out of the refrigerator.

"What's going on?" I asked.

"Your father has officially been cleared."

"What?"

"I told you, Maya, sweetie, there was nothing to worry about," my dad said. "My CFO admitted what he did in exchange for a lighter sentence. He told them I wasn't involved, so they finally dropped the charges."

"So all is well in the Morgan household," my mom said.

I watched them toast, clinking their glasses. If only they knew, all was far from well. At least for me. But I'd have to wait another day before telling them my drama. I couldn't burst their bubble right now. Somebody in the Morgan family needed to experience a little happiness.

Chapter 37

I slowly chewed the last of my Belgian waffle. Usually, I didn't eat such a heavy breakfast, but our housekeeper, Sui, made the best homemade waffles, and I just wanted to indulge. I'd double up on the Pilates later.

"Miss Maya, there's someone at the gate for you," Sui said, appearing in the kitchen.

"Who?" I asked, looking up from my plate.

"I think your friend, from your show?"

I had no idea who she was talking about. She knew Sheridan by name, so she would've just said her name. I got up and made my way over to the security monitor. I pressed the button and was shocked to see Shay at the gate. She was alone in her white Range Rover.

"Hey, Shay," I said hesitantly.

She leaned out the window and talked to the camera. "What's up, Maya? I need to talk to you."

"Shay, I'm not in the mood for any drama."

"Girl, ain't nobody trying to get caught up in any drama. I thought about what you said, and I believe you, that Jayla is behind it all."

"What? What changed your mind?"

She let out a long sigh. "I overheard her bragging to that geek she hangs with at school about making life miserable for you. Told the girl that she filed a restraining order because you were stalking her. I knew she was lying then. Just let me in."

Nothing anyone could tell me about Jayla surprised me anymore. I pressed the button to buzz Shay in and was waiting with the front door open by the time she made her way up my walkway.

"Girl, I don't know how you manage to keep hooking up with these psychopaths," she said, walking in. She tossed her oversized Chanel bag on my sofa and plopped down. "Something is wrong with that girl."

"Yeah, she definitely is crazy. At first, I thought she was just a superfan, but it's like her beef with me is personal. She's setting out to destroy my life."

"Well, in the process of trying to destroy your life, she's messing with mine, and I don't play that."

I smiled. "So are you going to help me?"

She rolled her eyes, but said, "What do I need to do?"

A wave of relief passed through me. I didn't know if this would work, but at this point, it was my only shot.

"We need someone who can get close to Jayla. She thinks you don't like me."

Shay laughed. "I don't."

I smiled at her and wanted to tell her that the feeling was mutual, but I kept my mouth closed. "Well, that makes you perfect to get next to her."

"And what am I supposed to do once I get close to her?"

"Play up how you don't like me and see if she'll admit anything to you."

"She's not going to tell me anything," Shay said doubtfully.

"You said yourself, Jayla has some kind of vendetta against me. If you can play up, I think she'll admit it."

"Un-unh," Shay said, shaking her head. "What's Plan B?"

I didn't need her negativity, but if she wasn't feeling the plan, I needed to move on to the next plan.

I sighed. "Well, another option is to get her to let you use her laptop."

"Use it for what?"

"If you can just get on it, I can give you a website to go to, to verify the IP address of that computer. Take a screen shot, and bam! I have my proof."

Shay must've been leaning toward that idea, because she slowly nodded. "Okay, *that* I may be able to do." She looked at me and added, "I'm helping you, but I still can't appreciate what you did."

"I know. Thank you, and I'm really sorry, again."

She finally gave me a genuine smile. "I could get used to this."

"Used to what?" I said.

"Maya Morgan apologizing to me."

"Oh, no, don't get carried away. It won't happen again."

We laughed, and we continued plotting to bring Jayla down.

Chapter 38

Operation Bust Jayla Cooper was in full effect.

That's why I was readying myself for the showdown with Shay. We'd decided that another public fight was exactly what we needed to get Jayla on Shay's side.

I don't know how Shay had gotten Jayla to sit with her at lunch, but there the two of them were. And right on cue, Shay shot me an evil look as I passed by. Jayla glared at me as well.

"Take a picture; it lasts longer," I said, stopping and striking a pose.

Shay stood up. "You got one more time to say something to me."

I took a step toward her table. "Or what? You gonna get this freak to hack into my email account?" I said, pointing to Jayla.

"Maya, that song is so played. And if I were you, I would watch what I say too, because I'd hate to have you arrested for harassing me." Jayla smirked, and it took everything in my power not to smack her upside her head.

"You don't get to talk to me at all," I said, holding my

hand up. "And you," I said, turning back to Shay, "need to head on back to the hood."

"Didn't you get the memo? I bought the hood."

"I'm so sick and tired of you." I took another step toward her. I hoped that we didn't have to get physical. The plan was for Evian to step in and stop us, but she was nowhere to be found.

Luckily, the vice principal, Mrs. Young, passed our table. "I know you two are not about to go at it again." She pointed at me. "Miss Morgan, keep it moving."

I rolled my eyes at Jayla and Shay. "You both are losers. Birds of a feather," I said, walking off.

I took a seat at a table a few rows over. I don't know what Shay was saying, but she and Jayla were deep in conversation. The plan had been for Shay to convince Jayla to let her use her laptop, saying hers was dead and she needed to finish her homework and email it. Shay was going to say that she wanted to do it right there in the cafeteria so Jayla wouldn't suggest that she go to the computer lab. I hoped the plan worked, because Plan C was just to beat Jayla to a pulp and get her to leave me alone that way.

Chapter 39

Done! Sent screenshot to your new email address.

I was so happy to see that text from Shay. She hadn't been able to get on the laptop at lunch, because Jayla didn't have it with her. So, she'd invited Jayla over this evening and then pretended something was wrong with her laptop. I hadn't known if that was going to work, but from this text message, it had!

I was going to take this information to the cops, and, hopefully, this nightmare would soon be over.

I grabbed some fruit, sat down at the bar in the kitchen, and flipped on the television. As usual, it was on my station, but I wasn't ready for what I saw.

"What's up, everyone, and welcome to *Rumor Central.* There's a new diva dishing the dirt."

I couldn't tear my eyes away from my television.

"I'm Ariel Edwards, and I'll be filling in while my girl, Maya Morgan, deals with some personal drama. But don't worry, I got the scoop."

I wanted to scream as I watched Ariel. I couldn't believe they were even giving her the time of day. She had nothing on me, except a couple of years.

I don't even know what story she was doing, because I was in my car, heading to the station, before the first commercial break. The show had been taped earlier in the day (I could tell it was taped because they had to use a 'pre-taped' disclaimer in the opening credits). I guess they didn't trust Ariel to go live, so I wasn't sure if she would even still be there. And I knew that I didn't want any problems, so I was going to wait for her outside. But I needed to make it very clear that she would not be taking my job.

I parked across the street from the station and waited. I didn't see her car, so I called the front desk and asked to speak to her. When the receptionist transferred me and I heard Ariel say hello, I hung up. So she was still there.

I continued waiting and, about thirty minutes later, saw Ariel come out. I expected her to go to the side parking lot, where the employees parked, but she walked straight down the front walkway and stopped as a car pulled up to the curb.

"Wait, is that . . ." I leaned in so I could get a closer look. "That's Jayla!"

Ariel got in the car, and they took off. I followed, while dialing Tamara's cell phone number at the same time.

"Hello, Tamara," I said after she picked up.

"Hey, Maya, still no news, but I'm working on it," she said.

"No, that's not why I'm calling," I said. "I thought Jayla was fired."

"She is. It hurt my heart to let her go, but with all this drama going on with her, I agreed; we couldn't keep her around."

"So, she's not working for Ariel?"

"Working for Ariel doing what?"

"I don't know. I just saw the two of them leave the station."

"Maya, what are you doing at the station?"

"I didn't come into the station. I was just passing by, and I saw the two of them together," I lied.

"I have no idea why the two of them are together. Jayla is no longer affiliated with WSVV," Tamara replied.

"Okay, thanks," I said, hanging up the phone before she could ask me any more questions.

I followed Jayla and Ariel for about ten more minutes, then watched as they pulled onto the campus of the University of Miami. That was Ariel's school, so Jayla must've been dropping her off. But I couldn't understand what they were doing together. In Jayla's entire time at the station, she had never let on that she even knew Ariel.

I watched as they parked, then went inside one of the dorms. I whipped into a handicapped space, jumped out, and discreetly followed them inside. Ariel had probably hired the girl to get some publicity on social media.

I felt like a spy as I blended in with the group of sorority girls walking into the building. I was close enough to see Ariel and Jayla, but far enough away, and mixed up with all the other girls, that they were unlikely to see me.

"I just saw you on TV," some girl said to Ariel.

"You said you were going to make it happen. Go, diva!" another one said.

"And I always do what I say," Ariel replied.

"Hey, Jayla," the girls said to her, which meant they must know her, too.

Now, my curiosity was definitely piqued.

"I'm going to run in my room and change and we can go," I heard Ariel tell Jayla.

"Yeah. Since I can't stand your roommate, I'll wait out here," Jayla said. She said something else I couldn't make out, before walking over to a sofa by the mailboxes. I watched Ariel go into the first door in the long hallway off the common area.

I ducked into the bathroom so I wouldn't be spotted. Some girl stared at me, so I pulled out my phone and acted like I was in an intense argument.

She stopped being nosey and stepped in the stall to use the restroom. I couldn't go out yet, so I pretended I was continuing the conversation.

"I just can't believe you would do this me," I fake cried.

She walked back out and, again, looked my way as she washed her hands. I prayed she didn't recognize me, but since my hair was pulled back in a ponytail and I was looking less fabulous than I'd looked in a long time, maybe she wouldn't.

"Girl, dry your tears. No guy is worth it." She wiped her hands, then walked out of the restroom.

After she left, I poked my head back out. I saw a seat on the other side of the large common room and quickly darted over there. Thankfully, this place was so cluttered and people were everywhere. I wanted to be out of view, but still able to see when Ariel came out, which she did about ten minutes later. She and Jayla exited out the front double doors.

I considered following them, but I thought I'd have a better shot of getting answers from her roommate. So, I chilled for a little while longer, just to be safe. When I was sure they were gone, I went and knocked on the door to Ariel's room.

"What?" the girl said, opening the door. She looked like something out of a vampire movie. She had long, stringy black hair, black nails, and was dressed in all black.

"Hey, I'm Ariel's cousin, ummm . . . Vanilla."

"Vanilla?"

I shrugged, kicking myself that that dumb name was the best I could come up with. "Yeah, I know. My mom was high on painkillers or something. Ariel sent me back to her room to get her jump drive."

"Fine," the girl said, leaving the door open for me to come in.

I walked into the room and shut the door. "How are you?" I asked her as she sat back down on her bed.

She cut her eyes at me, put her earphones over her ears, and said, "I'm studying."

That let me know she didn't feel like being bothered. That was fine by me.

"She said she left it over by her desk," I said out loud anyway. The girl kept ignoring me. I looked around Ariel's desk. I didn't know what I was looking for, other than answers. I saw stacks of demo tapes and her resume. I picked her resume up. This heffa had changed her job description already. Under *Rumor Central*, she had "host."

I looked some more, then stopped cold when I saw a picture of Jayla hanging on a corkboard over her desk. Why would Ariel have a picture of Jayla? I glanced back to see if the roommate was paying me any attention. She wasn't, so I eased the photo off the corkboard and turned it around to see if anything was on the back.

To the best sister in the whole wide world. Love you, Jayla.

I had to catch my balance, I was so stunned. They were sisters! These heffas had played me, and I had fallen for it hook, line, and sinker.

Chapter 40

Things couldn't have come together better if I'd written the script myself. I had been all prepared to give my "Please give me an extension" speech, when Alvin's words popped into my head: *All this research you're doing, that's your paper right there.*

He was right, and I'd started writing, and before I knew it, my ten-page paper was done. I'd learned so much over these last few weeks, and that had made this one of the easiest projects I'd ever done. I'd knocked it out in less than two hours and had decided on the perfect payback plan while I was at it.

My English teacher, Mrs. Williams, stood at the front of the crowded classroom. All three English classes had come together for the research paper presentations, so the classroom was packed. "So, who would like to go first?" she asked.

I raised my hand. "I would."

Mrs. Williams wasn't the only one surprised. Several of my classmates looked at me crazy as well.

"Miss Morgan, so you've actually completed your assignment?" she asked.

"I sure have," I said with a grin. "It's fab if I must say so myself."

"Well, I'm glad that you're confident, and, may I say, this is a first, so I am more than honored to have you take the floor."

She pointed to the front of the room, then went and sat down off to the side to watch my presentation.

The presentation equipment was all ready to go, so all I had to do was plug my laptop in. I turned my computer on and waited for my report to appear on the large screen Mrs. Williams had set up for us at the front of the room.

The words *Digital Bandits* appeared across the screen.

"My report today is on Digital Bandits."

The teacher stood up. "Okay, Miss Morgan, let me stop you. You do know your research paper is supposed to be on a topic that will inform and educate your classmates?"

"Oh, trust me, Mrs. Williams. Everyone will be more than informed when I'm done." I flashed my signature smile.

I turned back to the class. "I know a lot of you communicate now via social media, all out in the open. But raise your hand if you still send emails, or private messages, or direct tweets that you wouldn't exactly want others to see."

Most of the people in the class held up their hands.

"The digital age is here to stay," I continued. "That's why you have to protect your privacy, or you could find yourself in a big cyber mess. Think you're safe because you have virus protection or you don't share your passwords?" I looked directly at Jayla, who was sitting in the row closest to the door. "And if you do share your passwords, you quickly change them when you realize some freak might have gotten ahold of them."

She just glared at me. I guess she wasn't feeling my presentation.

"Another question: How many of you store your passwords? You know how your computer says 'do you want to remember this password.' Any of you do that?"

More people raised their hands.

"Did you know that's like leaving the key in the front door of your house?"

I spouted off a whole lot of other statistics and stuff I'd learned in my quest to track down my hacker. I had every ear in the class. Everyone was paying attention to my presentation, even Mrs. Williams. This was one homework assignment I hadn't minded doing. Of course Alvin had helped me out with a lot of it, but I'd done a whole lot of research on my own. Then, it had all come together so perfectly.

"And if you don't think a cybercrime can happen to you, let me show you how it can." I clicked some more buttons on the computer. "This is my email account." I pointed to the screen. "Don't worry, I'm going to change it after this presentation." I laughed. "But someone actually remotely accessed my computer. That means, they weren't in my house when they hacked into my computer system and basically took it over."

"That doesn't even make sense," one of my classmates said. "Nobody can do that."

"That's what I used to think . . . until someone did it to me." I looked at Jayla again, and although she was trying to act all non-fazed, I could see the tension in her face.

"At first, I was a little upset, thinking there was nothing I could do," I continued. "I mean, how can you catch a cyber criminal? But I was wrong."

I pushed a button to go to another screen. It showed a blurry picture of a girl behind bars.

"Is . . . is that . . ." One of my classmates peered at the screen, then back at Jayla. "Is that *her?*"

"Of course it's not me," Jayla snapped, more shaken than she wanted to let on.

I just smiled and kept talking. "Cyber crime is a felony,

and you can go to jail." I spoke slowly and looked directly at Jayla. She diverted her eyes down, like something on her desk was really interesting her. I bet she wished she'd never transferred to Miami High now.

"People are always playing around online," one of my classmates said. "What if we just say it was a prank?"

"Well, lots of people try to use that defense, but it never stands up in court," I replied.

"Someone could always say it wasn't him," someone else said.

"They can say what they want, but just like each of us has a unique fingerprint"—I held up my perfectly manicured index finger—"the cyber world has unique digital footprints. So anything you send can be traced."

I changed the screen to show a long number. "You see this number? It's called an IP address. This is the footprint of my hacker."

Several people gasped. "That's right. I know who hacked me, pretending to be me as she sent out horrible emails in my name, harassed me, and tried to get me fired from my job."

"Who?" someone yelled.

I hit another button, and Jayla's picture popped up.

"It *is* her!" the guy yelled.

"Are you crazy?" Jayla said.

"Nope, but you must be," I coolly replied.

"You are on some kind of drugs!" Jayla snapped.

"We know you hacked into my account."

Even Mrs. Williams must've been caught up in the drama, because she was looking back and forth between us like it was a tennis match.

"Yeah, that's the song you've been singing for weeks," Jayla said.

"And I don't have to sing it anymore. We have proof. Your IP address has been traced, Dumbo. And just so you know, I have turned it over to the police."

That made her nervous. "I didn't do anything."

"Okay, keep denying it, but we have proof. So that's all that matters."

"Why would I do something like that?"

"Hmmmm, let's see, maybe because your *sister*, Ariel, wanted to replace me on *Rumor Central,* and you were going to help her. Maybe both of you just wanted me out of the way. I don't know. You claimed to be a fan, but it was all some kind of scam. But now, the scam's on you."

Jayla glared at me. "You think you're so high and mighty. Yeah, I was a fan. I was a fan till I got to know you and learned how you treated my sister. Nobody messes with my family like that!" she blurted out.

Mrs. Williams must've snapped out of her shock, because she jumped up and finally said, "Okay, that's enough!"

Jayla grabbed her purse and headed to the door. "I'm outta here."

"Ummm, not so fast," the police officer who met her at the door said.

Jayla's mouth dropped open as she backed up in shock.

"Jayla Cooper?" he asked.

She didn't say a word, but I answered. "That's her."

"You are under arrest."

"Arrest, for what?" she cried.

"Identity theft, unauthorized use of a computer."

Jayla tried to push past the cop. "I didn't do anything."

The officer pulled her hands behind her back. "You have the right to remain silent. . . ."

I heard her cursing and crying as they pulled her out into the hallway. My dad had had to pull some strings to get an of-ficer on the case so quickly, but with the evidence Shay got and that Alvin had compiled, the police were able to tie Jayla to all the hacking in my email account and the hijacking of my info. I had finally told my dad, and he had had his security people do a scan of our computers. Turns out Jayla had logged into my family's bank account. I don't know if she was just being nosey or had actually planned to steal something. She hadn't been able to take anything, because my dad has all kinds of security measures, but that added a wire fraud charge. After that, my dad was all too happy to call in favors to get his cop friend on the case ASAP. My dad had gotten the money laundering charges against him dismissed, but he said the article in the *Enquirer* had been "bad for business," so he definitely wasn't happy to know that it had come about because Jayla had hacked into our computers.

I gathered my things as my classmates kept buzzing. "Mrs. Williams, is it okay if I leave? I need to go handle some business."

She nodded, but followed me outside into the hall. "Miss Morgan, great presentation. But really, did you have to be so dramatic? Couldn't you just have turned the girl in?"

"Now, Mrs. Williams, you know how I roll. When Maya Morgan does something, she does it up big." I felt like a weight had been lifted off my shoulders. I was sure this whole story was going viral at that very moment.

She smiled and shook her head. "Guess I do know that."

"But the bigger question is, do I get an A?"

She nodded. "Of course you do. I think we all were more than informed. I'll even be changing my password as soon as class is over."

It was my turn to smile. A good grade AND Jayla was out of my hair? Oh yeah, today was a good day.

Chapter 41

It felt so good to be back. I had called Tamara to tell her about Jayla's arrest, and she told me the investigation had wrapped up, too, because they concluded Jayla was behind the Daysia story, so I could come back to work. So instead of going home, I made a beeline to the station.

I was in my office when I heard Ariel's voice, obviously talking to someone on the phone. "I told you, girl, it's a new diva in town." Ariel stopped in the doorway when she noticed me sitting at my desk. She froze with her phone still to her ear. "Ummm, hey, Lisa, let me call you back." She hung up the phone.

"H-hey, Maya. What's going on?" she said, slowly walking into the room.

I leaned back in my chair. "What does it look like?"

"What are you doing here? Why aren't you in school?"

"I left early," I said. "Why?"

"No, I was just wondering, you know, why you were here."

"I work here."

The look on her face was priceless.

"Oh, what, you weren't expecting me to come back?" I asked.

"No, of c-course I was," she stammered. "I just didn't—"

"I told you it was just temporary."

"I know, but well, I thought you know with Daysia . . ."

I slammed my hand down on the desk. "You thought that you would give me the bogus story on Daysia, and you knew I wouldn't follow through and check it, and you used it to your advantage. Yeah, that's my fault, and I paid for that." I stood and slowly walked from behind my desk. "But I've learned a valuable lesson, a few actually. Number one, always verify things myself. And number two, be careful whom you trust. So, now I know."

Ariel shifted uncomfortably. "So, ah . . . um . . . welcome back." She looked around the room. "So, does that mean . . ."

"What, that you won't be doing the show tonight?"

She stared at me blankly.

"No, you won't be doing *my* show. Not tonight, tomorrow, or ever again."

"What is that supposed to mean?"

"You set me up. You think I'm gonna let you keep working here? I've already talked to Tamara." It gave me great pleasure to utter my next words. "You're fired."

"Are you kidding me? I didn't have anything to do with any of this. I'm just as shocked as you that the story was bogus," she said defiantly.

"Tell that to someone else," I said. "You and your *sister* have been working together from day one."

She had the nerve to look confused. I guess this chick was gonna play her deception to the end. "S-sister, what sister? What are you talking about?"

"Don't play me, Ariel. Your sister, Jayla." I looked her up and down. "Now that I think about it, she was at the mall when I did the personal appearance. Was she there with you?

Did you guys pay that creep to attack me in the restroom? Was this all some elaborate scheme?"

"You are truly crazy," she said. "Her name is Jayla Cooper. I'm Edwards."

"So you have different last names. Your mama got around."

She flinched, but stood her ground. "I didn't know Jayla before working here. You are being your usual dramatic self."

I leaned back against the wall and folded my arms across my chest. "Oh, then I guess you don't care that Jayla was arrested a couple of hours ago and is now down at Miami PD waiting to be booked on felony identity theft, computer hacking and wire fraud charges."

If there was ever any doubt, it was all erased by the look of horror on her face.

"What?" Ariel exclaimed.

"Yeah, your little sister was arrested. And if I have my way, you'll be next!"

"Oh, my, God, what did you do?" she cried, turning and racing from my office.

"Just showed you what happens when you mess with Maya Morgan," I called out after her.

I turned the music up on my iPhone and started singing as I got ready for my comeback show.

Chapter 42

Life could be so funny sometimes. That's all I could think as I sat at the high table in the corner of the Grand Ballroom at the Hilton Hotel. Our winter dance was going strong, and although this was no longer my scene, I had decided to show up just to get out of the house—and not to mention the extra credit points that I desperately needed. Because attendance had been so down at all these parties, the teachers had taken to giving us extra credit if we attended and stayed at least an hour. And since Mr. Patton, my calculus teacher, was watching me, I had forty-five minutes to go.

But it was all good. Of course I was getting my shine as always, with everyone coming up and talking to me about Jayla. I didn't know where she would be graduating from, but it definitely wouldn't be Miami High. If I had my way, it could be the state pen, but they said at most, she'd face some misdemeanor fraud charges. But the most important thing was I'd gotten her out of my life. And I knew the Internet wasn't going anywhere, but you'd better believe I was going to be a whole lot more protective and careful when I was online. Jayla had tried to ruin my life, and she'd almost succeeded, but good thing she didn't know me like that.

I also wanted to see how far that skank, Ariel, was going to get in this business. It would be interesting to see where she landed. But after I got through blackballing her, hopefully she'd land in the gutter. Yeah, I knew I should take the high road and leave her alone. But . . . NOT!

"Maya, you heard what I said?"

I had been so lost in my thoughts; I had forgotten Bryce was standing in front of me, giving me some whack apology.

"I'm sorry, what were you saying?" I asked.

He shifted. "I was just saying you're looking real good."

I wanted to laugh. But I just took a sip of my drink. "I know."

He smiled his half smile. "Well, I'm sorry I didn't believe you."

"It's all good," I said, stopping him. "It just showed me you don't really know me."

"Come on, Maya," he said. "It's not like that. I said I'm sorry." He hesitated. "I really miss you. I was hoping we could pick up where we left off."

I could only shake my head. "Nah, I'm straight. Let's just leave it alone."

He looked dejected. "Can we at least be friends?"

"I don't need any new friends, Bryce."

He blew a frustrated breath. "So how long are you going to have an attitude?" he asked.

"I'm not mad at you. You do you, and I'll do me." I really didn't have an attitude with Bryce. He'd turned on me. Twice. He wouldn't get another chance.

"Seriously, Maya?"

Our conversation was interrupted by loud, piercing screams. Both Bryce and I looked in the direction where the screams were coming from. We didn't know what all the commotion was, but the girls were going crazy.

I noticed Darrell first, as he pushed his way through the

crowd. I almost fell out of my seat when J. Love walked up to my table.

"What's up, ma?" he said, then turned and noticed Bryce. "Excuse me, man. Can I holla at my girl in private real quick?"

Bryce looked at him, then at me, then at Darrell, before stomping off without saying a word.

I crossed my legs but stayed quiet.

"Dang, you're looking good," J. Love said.

"I know." Could these dudes really not come up with any better lines?

Darrell was trying to keep the girls at bay, but J. Love didn't seem fazed. All his attention was on me.

"And to what does Miami High owe the honor of the great J. Love passing through its winter party?" I asked.

He laughed. "Oh, trust and believe, I'm here for one reason, and one reason only."

"And what would that be?"

"I had some real important business to handle."

"Don't you always?"

I couldn't help it. *Him,* I had a serious attitude with. I understood his being mad because of what he thought I did, but to not even give me a chance to be heard? That was foul. He had treated me like some chicken-head groupie, and I wasn't going to forget that so quickly.

"Well, look here. I saw the news article about everything that happened to you. Sorry I didn't believe you."

I shrugged but didn't reply.

"Can we go somewhere and talk?"

"We're talking now."

He looked around the hotel. "Yeah, but this ain't really my crowd."

I held my hand out and pointed in the direction he came from. "Well, the door is that way."

"Come on, Maya. I know I was a little hard on you, but I thought you had sold me out."

"I told you I didn't." I mean, I know I told Kennedi, but that didn't count.

"Yeah, but you know, I didn't know you like that, and I just didn't—"

"You're right. You didn't know me, and you refused to hear me. You said it yourself, we had a connection, yet you refused to hear anything I had to say. But it's all good." I looked him up and down. "I understand you superstars gotta play it safe."

He stepped closer to me and rubbed my thigh. "Come on, baby. You're a star, too, and you know we look good together."

"Yeah, until the next time something happens to make you doubt me and you can't even bother to hear my side."

"I apologized for that." He actually looked like he was getting a little frustrated. "And you know I don't do this. I don't chase after no girl."

I cut my eyes at him. "Did I ask you to come here? No, I didn't. So feel free to use the exit at any time."

He stopped and laughed. "Girl, you're some kind of fire-cracker. Come on; let's get out of here. Let me go make it up to you."

He reached for my arm, which I jerked out of his way. "Yeah, sorry, I'm not going to be able to do that. I don't want to leave my date."

"What, ol' boy who just left? Your kinda sorta man?"

"Oh no." I shrugged nonchalantly. "Bryce is history."

"Then what's the problem?"

"I have a date, and I'm not about to leave him and go run off, not even with the great J. Love." I motioned to all the girls behind him, looking like they were about to pass out. "I'm sure you can have your pick of any girl in this room, so

I'm sure you'll be okay." I stood. "So, if you'll excuse me, here's my date."

J. Love's mouth dropped open as the tall, lanky guy stepped up to me. "You have got to be kidding me?"

"Hello," Alvin said, pushing his glasses up on his nose.

"Come on, Maya. Are you for real?" J. Love asked.

I just stood there, smiling. Alvin had cleaned up well. With the exception of that tweed blazer and those Coke bi-focals, he didn't look half bad. After all he'd done to help me, I figured the least I could do was invite him to the dance as a way of saying thanks. And he'd shown up like a real gentle-man, complete with a town car and roses. He had come in to meet my dad. Of course, my mom had been horrified, but at least she wasn't rude. I'm sure she was going to be waiting at home to hear all about how I hooked up with Alvin. But it wasn't even like that. I was still Maya Morgan, after all. I just wanted to give ol' Alvin a bright spot in his life by going out with him.

"I'm Alvin," he said, sticking his hand out for J. Love to shake. J. Love just stared at him. Alvin dropped his hand, un-fazed.

"Maya, you not gonna introduce me to your friend, since he's being quite rude?" Alvin said.

"Umm, yeah, this is J. Love. He's a singer."

Alvin grinned at J. Love. "Oh, well, isn't that special. I've never heard of you, but you keep at it. I'm sure you're tal-ented and can grow up to be like Chris Brown or something one day." He patted J. Love on the shoulder. "Excuse me now. This is Maya's song, so we're gonna go dance."

He took my hand and led me away.

I will never forget the look on J. Love's face, and Alvin didn't know it, but he had just earned major cool points.

J. Love was more my speed. And since Maya Morgan didn't do nerds, maybe I'd forgive him later. For now, though, I wanted to see him squirm. I noticed him standing there watching me with a smile while I danced with Alvin.

Finally, J. Love walked off, passing by me on the dance floor on his way out. He leaned in and whispered, "You're a piece of work, girl. But we *will* see other again."

I was about to say something when Alvin leaned in and whispered, "But it won't be tonight, bruh. So keep it moving."

I loved it! Alvin was showing me a whole new side. I just might have to get to know him a little bit better.

That's the beauty of being Maya Morgan. I had options, and a girl could never have too many of those.

YOU DON'T KNOW ME LIKE THAT

ReShonda Tate Billingsley

ABOUT THIS GUIDE

The following questions are intended to
enhance your group's reading of
YOU DON'T KNOW ME LIKE THAT.

DISCUSSION QUESTIONS

1. With Maya's being a celebrity, do you think she was too trusting of the people she let into her inner circle? What could she have done to be more careful?

2. Maya's unwillingness to help Ariel is what sparked all of her troubles. Do you think Maya should have helped Ariel? Why do you think she didn't?

3. Bryce was furious when the fans approached Maya during their intimate dinner. Do you think he was right to get upset? How should Maya have handled the situation?

4. What were some warning signs that Maya should have seen, clueing her in to the fact that Jayla was her stalker?

5. Both J. Love and Bryce were quick to believe the worst about Maya. Should she forgive them, or should she give Alvin a chance? Which guy would you like to see her with?

6. Maya ultimately had to turn to Shay to help her catch her stalker. Do you think Shay should've helped?

7. Have you ever had someone stalk/harass you online? How did you handle it?

8. What efforts do you take to protect your information when you're online?

Rumor Central continues with
As Real As It Gets.

Coming in January 2014.
Wherever books and eBooks are sold!

The image on the screen gave me chills.

I knew Savannah Vanderpool. She was a beautiful, former Miss Teen Miami who had branched out to movies. We'd taken some modeling classes together when I was in middle school, and although I didn't talk to her much now, we kept in touch through Instagram and Twitter. It wasn't often that I gave other girls props. But Savannah had earned hers. She was Beyoncé, Ciara, and Megan Goode rolled up into one. A class act, that's who Savannah was.

Was.

Because this chick I was looking at right now was anything but classy. She looked like a crackhead, methhead, and dope fiend rolled up into one.

Savannah's eyes were sunken, almost like her face was swallowing them. She had dark circles around her eyes, and her face was taut and dry. Her once beautiful blond hair was stringy, and the dark roots were showing.

"Maya," my director, Manny, whispered in my ear. "Go! You're live!"

I caught myself. I didn't usually let anything get me off my game when I was in hosting mode at my talk show, *Rumor*

Central, but seeing Savannah's picture had definitely left me speechless.

"Wow, I guess you can say I'm a little stunned myself," I continued, turning my attention back to the camera. "If you knew Savannah Vanderpool like I knew Savannah Vanderpool, you'd be just as shocked, too," I spoke to the camera.

We'd gotten the story about Savannah's being arrested just minutes before I was going on the air. My producer, Dexter, had handed me a sheet with some limited information and told me to wing it. I had no problem with that, because dishing dirt was what had made me so popular on *Rumor Central.* I was even used to dishing dirt about my friends, especially because I was usually the one who had dug up the dirt. Even though I'd stopped airing my friends' dirty laundry, I had no problem digging in other celebrities' backyards. I had to. Since I had started *Rumor Central* a few months ago, it had become one of the hottest gossip shows in the country. We were syndicated, and my popularity was through the roof. Celebs as big as Usher and Rihanna called me when they wanted to "slip" out a little gossip, and other celebrities tried to become my best friends to keep their dirt off the air. So, a little scandalous story never shocked me. But this picture of Savannah . . . I wasn't ready for that.

"This is just in to the *Rumor Central* studios," I continued, "so we haven't been able to get all the details, but rumor has it that this mug shot is from Savannah's arrest last night, after she caused a scene at the *Sports Illustrated* reception when organizers saw her and refused to let her go on stage. We're told Savannah was so high that she took off all her clothes and began running through the party screaming and crying as she destroyed everything in sight."

I took a deep breath as an earlier photo of Savannah as Miss Teen Miami flashed on the screen.

"Apparently, Savannah was high on K2, a hyped up version of Kush, the popular synthetic drug sweeping the country. We don't know much about K2, but you'd better believe that *Rumor Central* is all over this story, and we'll keep you updated. I'm your girl, Maya Morgan, and we'll be back right after this."

I tossed to the break and motioned for my new assistant, Yolanda, to get me some water. Usually, we kept it light and gossipy on *Rumor Central*. I didn't get all deep into stories, and this was exactly the reason why.

"You okay?" Yolanda asked as she handed me a chilled bottled water.

"Yeah, just trippin' over that picture." I glanced over at the photo, which was back up on the monitor. I'd seen Savannah about six months ago, and she had looked fine. How could someone fall off like that in just a few months?

Dexter came over to me on the set as Yolanda scurried away.

"Great job, Maya. I got some more details. Apparently, this K2 is more powerful than Kush and getting really hot among celebrities."

"Just wow," I said, shaking my head again at the picture. I knew some celebs who dabbled in drugs, but Savannah had done a lot more than dabble. "I just can't believe that she's fallen off like that."

"Do you know Savannah?" Dexter asked. "I mean, personally. I figured you did since you know everybody."

Dexter was right about that. Before I was on air—first as one of the five members of the *Miami Divas* reality show, then as the host of my own show—I had already been at the top of the food chain as the leader of Miami's "it" clique. In fact, that's why I'd been approached to do the reality show in the first place. That show hadn't done as well as they had wanted, so they'd canceled it, fired the other four divas, and had given me my own show. That had been the smartest thing since the invention of the Internet, because in no time I had become the go-to chick for all the latest celebrity gossip, dirt, and entertainment news. *Rumor Central* had exceeded everyone's expectations and been picked up by several other cities.

My BFF, Sheridan, had been one of the *Miami Divas* who was fired and that had led to a whole lotta drama, but we'd squashed that and were back to kickin' it. I couldn't say the same about the other busters from *Miami Divas*. Shay, Bali, and Evian still had stank attitudes about the way everything went down. (They claimed we had had a pact to stick together and I had sold them in taking my own show. As if any of them would've turned it down if the shoe had been on the other foot. Whatever.)

"So, do you know her or not?" Dexter asked again, snapping me out of my thoughts.

I knew he wasn't asking out of concern. He was probably trying to see if I could get some kind of inside scoop.

"Yeah, I know her. Or, at least I *used* to know her," I replied. "The Savannah I knew would never allow herself to look like this."

"The research department is trying to dig up info on this K2, but apparently, it is a powerful, addictive thing," Dexter said.

I didn't get it, because drugs were whack. Anything that took me off my A game, I didn't need to be doing. Savannah used to be the same way. Was this thing powerful enough to make her change her mind? I glanced at the picture again. Obviously, it was.